The Devil's Pit

and other stories

UNESCO COLLECTION OF REPRESENTATIVE WORKS:
LATIN AMERICAN SERIES. PUBLISHED WITH
THE COOPERATION OF THE
ORGANIZATION OF AMERICAN STATES.

The Devil's Pit

and other stories

by

Baldomero Lillo

Translated
by
Esther S. Dillon
and
Angel Flores

PAN AMERICAN UNION
GENERAL SECRETARIAT, ORGANIZATION OF AMERICAN STATES
WASHINGTON, D. C., 1959.

INTRODUCTION

I. Historical Background

In the South of Chile, near the dynamic and progressive city of Concepción, there is a coast very dramatic in its formations: there you can see hills with pine trees, luxuriantly green, covered by old ferns, sharp cliffs, soft hidden beaches washed by a tide thick with cochayuyo and other marine algae, peaceful fishing boats braided in a vast accumulation of nets. There the people go about their business in an atmosphere of quiet and detachment. Often they lose themselves among the solitary dunes. In certain zones gigantic constructions rise up where an activity reigns which the observer cannot immediately identify. At the top of some broad hills there is a fabulous park: Lota Park, and among the old native Chilean plants there is a magnificent mansion in the purest nineteenth century style. The mansion is permanently empty. It was never lived in by its owners. Through the paths in bloom you can see a pier. Immense machines convey, amid the din of cranes and chains, the cargo that the ships gradually swallow: black gold, Chilean coal. That empty mansion and that pier submerged in clouds of steam and soot are the symbols of a world that found its voice in the work of the most forceful writer in the expression of pathos that Chilean literature has produced: Baldomero Lillo.

That mining world as Baldomero Lillo knew it, was

for some time a source of great wealth which did not always contribute to the progress of the country. Its owners were eager for power and money so that they could become part of the luxurious decadent European world of the end of the nineteenth century. When they attempted to transport that luxury to their native soil and incrust it like a crown over the small black empire of their minerals, their country had already acquired a consciousness of its social and economic contradictions. Their attempt was in vain. It was anachronistic, almost suicidal. A short distance from the beautiful park and the princely mansion there existed a world of a different character, Dantesque in the extent of its misery: it was the world of the miners. There they lived in hovels pestilent and cramped, one on top of the other, sick, strangled by hunger. Their salaries were shameful and they had no social legislation to protect them. The law only protected the companies. The authorities winked in the face of these innumerable abuses. The government, far away, was busy playing politics rather than interesting itself in investigating conditions which, after all, it was not going to correct.

"To the coal producing region of Arauco," the distinguished essayist Ernesto Montenegro has written, "the flower of the youth has gone to waste away under the grinding stone of the harshest of all employment. In the days in which the author lives near them, the miners are confined just as they would be in a concentration camp. With virtuous prudence the Company has cut the communications with the outside world so that the workers may not fall into the temptations offered by 'dives' and gambling places. The Company made its own laws and coined its own money as if it were a foreign principality nailed on the margin of Chile. Fines and additional charges for materials completed the spoils and kept the worker in this way in forced slavery." [1]

[1] *De Descubierta.* Santiago de Chile, 1951, pp. 47-48.

A slave of the Company, the miner worked like a horse in submarine tunnels, risking his life every instant, under the threat of supporting wood, either worm eaten or insufficient, or the threat of the much feared highly explosive firedamp gas. Enchained by the debts contracted in the Company stores where he was forced to buy, the miner was never able to save enough to obtain his independence. He gave his life to the mine and in it he buried his family. Children began to work in mines at the age of ten or twelve. Once they had been dragged into the gloomy catacombs, their destiny was sealed.

Baldomero Lillo lived this hard life. He was not a miner, but he worked next to them as a clerk in the Company store. He responded to that social condition in a way that might be considered typical of his generation. Towards the end of the nineteenth century an industrial revolution took place which was to change the face of the Chilean nation. The repeated economic crises, the wasting of the nation's wealth, especially saltpeter, the absurd centralization that the government fostered, thus neglecting the fate of the provinces, and the absolute political domination that a privileged social class enjoyed caused the masses to look toward revolutionary programs set forth by European socialism and anarchism, and to become members of cultural and political institutions which in the long run accelerated the coming to power of the middle class of Chile. While the middle class was beginning to displace the upper class in the government, an upper class which was mostly a landowning class, the lower classes in the cities acquired a good measure of political power through syndicates, federations and associations with a very marked socialist tinge.

Baldomero Lillo, following very closely this revolutionary process, never went as far as to join any of these groups, but his sympathies, like those of the young intellectuals of 1910, were with the followers of the Liberal Alliance, the Radical Party and the Socialist Party. So great was the drama of these political struggles and the realism with which Lillo denounced to his country one aspect of the economic poverty and moral corruption which reigned that even today we usually identify his literary work with the saga of the coal miners. From this point of view, that is to say, considering Baldomero Lillo as a realistic writer fighting for the cause of the people, the historical background of his work is the revolutionary course that Chile followed from 1890 to 1920, more or less, a course in which, as has already been said, the middle class took over the government of the country, while the working class, especially that of the saltpeter districts of the North and the coal mines of the South, became aware of its political rights and organized in syndicates. Ideologically the new generations were inspired in the Socialist creed which had evolved from the mutualism of Francisco Bilbao[2] to dialectic Marxism. The First World War of 1914 and the Russian Revolution of 1917 were to play a decisive part in the political definition of those generations. But such events did not affect the work of Baldomero Lillo, who remained outside political activity all his life, inspired rather by a humanitarian zeal which led him to defend the principles of Christianity and social justice on a strictly idealistic plane.

II. Biographical Facts

The life of Baldomero Lillo has nothing of the spectacular about it. His was the obscure life of a man who consumed his revolutionary urges concentrating on the task of authentic writing. He was born on January 6, 1867 at the port of Lota. His parents were José Nazario Lillo and Mercedes Figueroa. Since his family was of modest means, he did not know the great ups and downs of fortune. His father continually felt the spurs of the desire of adventure and perhaps contributed to fire the

[2] A Chilean philosopher (1823-1865), author of *Sociabilidad Chilena*, founder of the Society for Social Equality (Sociedad de la Igualdad).

*imagination of his sons, while, by his example, he killed
in them any desire to imitate him. He tried everything
but had little success. In 1848 he was one of the first to
take part in the California Gold Rush. He returned after
two years with a treasure of anecdotes, but with his
pockets empty. Sitting at the family table he would read
history books and serials in newspapers. His children were
well nourished on all kinds of legends and folk tales.
Perhaps because they were apprehensive about their father's love of adventure, two of them decided very early
to become dreamers. Samuel became a poet; Baldomero,
a short story writer.*

*The early years of Baldomero have been recalled
by his brother Samuel in an interview which appeared
in the Chilean press a few years ago. Samuel says:*

"Baldomero had whooping cough as a child,
and this left him rather delicate. He was affected
by the smoke from the foundries that there are in
Lota where we were born and where my father was
employed by the Company. We studied at the
Lebu High School... We entered in 1883. Lebu
was a town which had just been founded, surrounded by trees, trees native to the region, not
planted by man. We lived at the foot of the mountain. Those were happy years for Baldomero who
became stronger. I remember that he used to go
hunting with my brother Fernando. My father had
a shotgun and a rifle. Fernando would take the rifle
and Baldomero, the shotgun. They would go hunting for wild pigeons, and they often shot some.
Baldomero was always the sharpshooter. With
powder they got from the mine and a receptacle of
my father's, they made bullets for the rifle. I saw
them myself grinding the thick black powder with
a bottle. His story, 'Shotgun' ('Cañuela y Petaca'),
is from beginning to end biographical. Baldomero
could not attend school regularly. He never grad-
uated."[3]

[3] "Mi hermano Baldomero Lillo: una entrevista a don Samuel
Lillo," *El Siglo* (Santiago de Chile, June 6, 1954).

*His bad health made regular study in high school
impossible. He was very young when he began to work
in the La Quincena store. At that time Lota had less
than six thousand inhabitants and lived by mining. When
his employers sent him to the nearby city of Concepción
to buy provisions for the store, Baldomero took advantage
of the opportunity to buy books. The Chilean writer
González Vera, zealous biographer of Baldomero Lillo,
recalls this episode in his study of Lillo in Sub Sole:*[4]

"In one of the first trips he acquired sketches
of life in old California by Bret Harte. He shared
with his brother Samuel the enthusiasm that he
felt on reading this book. On each trip he brought
back new books. In this way he read some books of
Pereda, Pérez Galdós, Dostoevski, Tolstoy and
Maupassant. He enjoyed Maupassant beyond all
measure. There was great pathos and great comedy
in his stories, and they were created almost out of
nothing. He possessed the gift of composition and
knew how to animate his stories."

*About this time he left his job at Lebu in order to
take charge of a store at the Buen Retiro mine, a league
from Coronel. He also married Natividad Miller. According to the words of his brother, it was here that he
began to feel the drama of the miners. Describing these
years of absorption for the writer, Samuel Lillo declares:*

"What decided his vocation as a writer was
his direct observation of the wretched life of the
miners in Lota. He was a penetrating observer of
life. He did not deal with great ideas nor great
philosophies, and he was outside politics and political parties. Above all he was interested in reality.
In Lota we would go down together into the mine.
I did this only three times; he, many more. He saw
at first hand what was happening there. He knew
'Gate Number 12' ('Compuerta número 12')... I
visited him at Buen Retiro. At that time I was living

in Santiago. He was an extremely avid reader. He used to take a trip to Concepción only to buy books. He had a Winchester and practiced shooting in the dunes, through which he would take long walks. In 1898, after an argument with the English manager of Buen Retiro, he came to Santiago."5

In Santiago, Baldomero Lillo tried many different types of employment. He was an insurance agent among other things. He finally established himself as an employee of the Council of University Extension, which was under the Secretariat of the University of Chile. His brother Samuel already enjoyed a solid literary prestige, and through him Baldomero came to know the great figures of Chilean literature of his day at meetings in Samuel's house, or at Diego Dublé Urrutia's, where the writers would read aloud their works and comment upon them. Baldomero would listen, and from time to time he would narrate in a conversational tone some dramatic incident he witnessed when he lived in Lota.

"He was a very talented storyteller"—his brother says—"it was delightful to listen to his stories. To convince him that he should write was very difficult. This idea first suggested itself in the meetings that took place at my home which were attended by Augusto Thompson, Ortiz de Zárate, Benito Rebolledo, Magallanes Moure, Francisco Santiván, Juan Francisco González, Diego Dublé. One day we listened to him tell 'Gate Number 12' ('La Compuerta Número 12'), and we begged him to write it down. Later I read it aloud in public at the Ateneo, because Baldomero would not dare. Some people doubted his existence and attributed to me the authorship of the story."6

And so, encouraged by his friends, Baldomero Lillo began to write his short stories. In 1903 he won a contest sponsored by the Revista Católica *with his story "Juan*

5 Samuel Lillo, *loc. cit.*
6 Samuel Lillo, *loc. cit.*

Fariña." By the following year he had gathered together enough stories for a volume. He could not find a title, however, until Diego Dublé came to his aid. "If all your stories take place in mines," they say he told him, "why don't you entitle the collection Sub Terra?"[7] The success of Sub Terra was extraordinary. The critics received it enthusiastically,[8] and in three months it was out of print. Shortly afterwards Lillo won a contest organized by the newspaper El Mercurio. He submitted a story which was to serve as the title of his second book: Sub Sole. Overnight he had become famous, and his fame did not remain in the literary circles, but spread throughout the country to be used as a weapon by the revolutionary students and workers.

In 1905, he moved to San Bernardo where he found a climate more suitable for his precarious health. There he gathered material for his famous story, "In the Cockpit" ("En la Rueda"). The consequence that this crude narration of a cockfight brought for him has been the theme of a colorful page by González Vera.[9] In 1907 he published his second book, Sub Sole, which, in spite of the praise of the critics, did not awaken the same enthusiasm as Sub Terra. The social conflicts in the saltpeter fields were increasing. The Socialists would have liked Baldomero Lillo to insist, as he did in his first book, on pathos. But the writer seemed eager to try out new themes in order to prove to the writers of his generation that he was also capable of using a purer style and of speculating with philosophical ideas in parables and allegories. A massacre of workers in the North, nevertheless, a-wakens in him again the desire for social redemption. He decides to write a novel about the exploitation suffered by the workers in the offices of the saltpeter companies.

[7] González Vera, op. cit., p. 209.
[8] Antonio Bórquez Solar, Federico Gana, Rafael Maluenda and Ignacio Pérez Kallens, among others, wrote about Sub Terra. See the bibliography of Baldomero Lillo compiled by González Vera, which appears in the 1943 edition of Sub Sole, in the appendix.
[9] González Vera, op. cit., p. 213.

The novel is to be called The Strike (La Huega). *He works carefully on its documentation. In 1909 he makes a trip to the North for the Council on Education. He talks to workers, gathers printed material, takes notes, and returns finally ready to complete his work. He writes one or two chapters which he reads and rereads, making many changes. This work becomes an obsession with him, but he is not able to carry it any farther. However, he never completely abandons the idea, although inside he knows that he will never be able to conclude it. He confessed to Eduardo Barrios: "I am not sufficiently acquainted with that environment... I have not assimilated it as I have that of the coal mines."*[10] *The Strike continued to plague him for the rest of his life, like a kind of literary mirage, nourished by his feelings of social solidarity but far away and out of reach.*

The truth is that Baldomero Lillo did not publish any other book after Sub Sole. *When he was able to forget his projected novel, he wrote short stories that the newspaper* El Mercurio *and the review* Zig-Zag *published immediately. In 1912 he lost his wife, and Lillo, whose health was steadily deteriorating, always on the verge of tuberculosis, had to take over the care of his four children. He retired in 1917 and from that time on he lived on his farm at San Bernardo taking care of a model chicken coop which he himself built to the admiration of his neighbors. There he received the periodic visits of his loyal friends. The great novelist Eduardo Barrios has left an unforgettable sketch of the retired Baldomero Lillo:*

"His weak constitution, that long body, ungainly, always in mourning; his thin face crowned with black hair, wiry, tossed like a sudden flash of fire and invaded by a sparse savage beard, stubble on poor land; his shoulders, high, angular, on which

[10] Eduardo Barrios, "Baldomero Lillo," *Revista Chilena* (XI, 1923), p. 416.

hung his jacket with only the top button fastened,
the bottom part falling open: then his trousers covering nothing but bones, with no form and always
short like those of an adolescent; finally his feet,
large, far apart, humble, feet with character. I see
him stand before my desk and repeat in silence his favorite movements: throwing his head
to one side, raising his hand with the fingers
stretched out and touching one another in order to
shake from a nostril some down or other, or some
imaginary dust; and continuing to chew something
feverishly afterwards. What? Nothing. It seems
that his nerves required him to accompany his inner
activity with that nervous habit of grinding down
his teeth."[11]

*He died on September 10, 1923, from tuberculosis.
In the summer of that year he had written his last story,
"Inamible," a masterpiece of Chilean humor.*

III. Sub Terra, 1904.

The first impression that the stories in Sub Terra
*produce can be deceiving. Their dramatic impact is so
strong, the reality of the environment so brutal, the
psychology of the characters so primitive and their defeat so simple in its fatalism that the reader, overwhelmed, thinks that he has had in his hands a direct,
unadorned, naked report of a detestable social situation.
Baldomero Lillo, it has been said, has done nothing more
than reproduce the observations that he accumulated
when he worked with coal miners. His work is nothing
more than a painful naturalistic document. Nevertheless, it is necessary to get over this first impression. The reader has to control his feelings of anger and
repulsiveness, to draw away from this mass of incidents
that fights to blind him and drown him with emotion, to
draw back and contemplate it in perspective. Then he*

[11] Quoted by González Vera, *op. cit.*, pp. 225-226.

begins to understand the true reality of the social phenomenon that preoccupies Lillo and the true nature of his
aesthetic expression.

From the outset we realize that his stories are not
"primitives," nor newspaper articles about the dramatic
life of the miner. On the contrary, they have gone
through a fine process of literary elaboration. The pathos,
the realism, the social criticism are deliberate. They fit
precisely into a form that represents tendencies dominant
in the epoch in which they were written. Whoever considers him a "primitive" because of his occasional errors
in grammar, besides mixing the problem of style with
that of language, cannot analyze the problems of literary
technique that Baldomero Lillo faced and solved, general-
ly, with success.[12] The stories in Sub Terra are evidently
part of the naturalistic tradition that comes to Chile from
France and Spain at the end of the nineteenth century.
Baldomero Lillo constructs after carefully studying the
works of his masters, of Zola especially. He is not careless
about the details. He uses the formula of the naturalists
and has perfect control over the multiple shades of their
colors. He always starts out with a definite situation which
might be of a social, moral or economic nature. He looks at
it from one angle, through a kind of hole that he drills
through the wall of reality, obtaining in this way a
deformed, partial picture, one that has the sordidness of
a nightmare and morbid pathos. He charges this situation with a thick emotional content and then hammers on
the feelings of the reader, arousing his sympathy, or
rather demanding it, unconditionally, by a process of

---

[12] Writers like Armando Donoso (Los Nuevos. Valencia, Spain,
1912, pp. 25-59) and Mariano Latorre (La Literatura Chilena. Buenos
Aires, 1941, pp. 146-147) criticised the defects of language in Lillo's
stories. There is authentic proof of the effort made by Lillo to make
the technical structure of his stories better. Examples of this are the
two versions he made of the same story: "The Hand that Stuck Fast"
("La Mano Pegada") and "The Vagabond" ("El Vagabundo"), as well
as the rewriting of a scene from "The Whale" ("La Ballena")—which
apparently he did not like—and which he inserted in another story
entitled "The Discovery" ("El Hallazgo").

accumulation which, since it takes us off guard, leaves us in a state of shock.

This wealth of emotion contrasts sharply with the cold objectivity that he shows in the description of the reality at hand. Baldomero Lillo presents his mining back-drops, the minutiae of life in a mining camp, the technical aspect of the subterranean work without wasting a detail. Rarely do you find mistakes in his minute graphic descriptions. His shortcomings when they exist are technical in character, and they are not the product of carelessness or of ignorance but, in my opinion, of excess of detail: for example, the superfluous recapitulation that interrupts the action of the stories "The Well" ("El Pozo") and "Searched" ("El Registro").

Alongside this contrast between objective realism and emotionalism, there is another contrast on a more abstract plane that might be defined as a play of light and shadow, of white and black. I do not know if Baldomero Lillo ever read the stories of Robert Louis Stevenson, a master of this stylistic device, but he did read Dostoevski and Pérez Galdós, and therefore he should have noticed the mysterious psychological quality that certain scenes described by them acquire by virtue of the fact that only two elements contend, the plane of concrete reality and the more intangible one of spiritual reality. The hero, pulled apart by the conflict between salvation and condemnation, seems to find the answer in the inanimate things that surround him, and he finds only a nightmarish repetition of the unknown in the light and shadow with which the surroundings affect him.[13] In the work of Baldomero Lillo this contrast often comes from the opposition of a poetic serenity in the landscape, which corresponds

[13] I will point out only two examples of this aspect of literary technique in the stories of Lillo. One in which the contrast of black against white is purely pictorial, just for the background, you might call it decorative. An example of this is "Pay Day" ("El Pago"). An example of the second aspect would be "The Devil's Pit" ("El Chiflón del Diablo"). Both stories are included in Sub Terra. There are also examples in Sub Sole: "In the Cockpit" ("En la Rueda"), for example.

to light, and a tragic situation, which is shadow. This is seen in "The Invalids" ("Los Inválidos"), "Pay Day" ("El Pago") and "The Devil's Pit" ("El Chiflón del Diablo").

In the development of his stories Lillo begins with a situation somewhat charged with emotion. The kernel of the narration is reached by means of a collective drama that suddenly becomes a crisis, and the denouement that follows is tragic. All Lillo's plots, with the exception of those in his humorous stories, consist of these three parts. The unity of Sub Terra is realized not only by the theme of the stories, but also by the narrative technique that is used in them. When the stylistic unity breaks and Lillo's style becomes mannered in his search for strange, elegant metaphors, it is possible that he is the victim of those writers of his generation who were closest to the modernista revolution. But this point needs a closer analysis. For the moment I shall limit myself to point to the marked influence of Rubén Darío that is found in certain landscape descriptions in Sub Terra and some classical allusions which against this mining camp backdrop are out of place. For instance, Lillo goes to the extreme of characterizing Petaca, a youth in one of his best stories, in these words: "Then the mighty Nimrod would shrug his shoulders disdainfully."

Nature in the stories in Sub Terra ranges from the unbridled pathos of "Gate Number 12" ("La Compuerta Número 12") and "Pay Day" ("El Pago"), from the dramatic, almost melodramatic, in "The Devil's Pit" ("El Chiflón del Diablo") and "Juan Fariña" to realistic observation tinged slightly by humor in "The Drill" ("La Barrena") and "The Shotgun" ("Cañuela y Petaca"). A story like "Firedamp" ("El Grisú") is weak because of oversimplification in the description of the villain, Mister Davis, which keeps it from being convincing. Another like "The Well" ("El Pozo") after a dramatic beginning falters because of the recapitulation that the author uses to identify the characters, but it picks up immediately and ends with a brutal denouement.

In order to appreciate these stories, the reader should realize that Baldomero Lillo is driven to write by an angelic anger. He has lived a drama which he considers not only shameful for his country but for all humanity. Here he has the example of Zola, whose novel Germinal made a profound impression on him, and of other crusaders of his generation who defended with equal ardor the rights of the classes that were being exploited. What is admirable in Sub Terra is the fact that the pathos, sometimes bordering on sentimentalism, never takes aways from the reality of the story, nor does it lessen the human warmth of the characters. If there is some artistic limitation in this work, it is not so much the result of its pathos as the rhetorical framework that the author imposed upon his work the moment he accepted the rigorous tenets of naturalism. This framework restricted the adventures of his imagination. Admiring the Russian novelists of the nineteenth century as he did, he was not as daring as they were in taking the step that was to free him from the commonplace and send him soaring into regions that were free, eccentric, mysterious, where he could have elucidated the spiritual conflicts of the individual as well as his enslaved social condition. Baldomero Lillo is so absorbed in finding ways to express the sordidness of his characters that his wings are clipped for flights of fancy, and he remains on earth, sub terra, surrounded by suffering men and women who seem to calm in him an obscure desire to suffer and feel compassion. On the ethical plane they compensate for what is sacrificed on the plane of poetry.

IV. Sub Sole, 1907.

In this work Baldomero Lillo abandons the mining theme almost completely and tries his hand in the world of the philosophic parable and the description of contem-

porary customs. In Sub Sole there are only two stories
related to the literature of social protest so characteristic of Sub Terra: "The Soul of the Machine" ("El
Alma de la Máquina"), set in a mining camp but not
"subterranean," since the man who works the machine,
the protagonist, manages from above the sinister routine
of the workers, and "Quilapán," a story of country life
in which the dramatic axis is the base exploitation of an
Indian by a white landowner.

It is interesting to observe how Lillo attains a finer
literary quality as soon as he breaks away from the obsessive naturalism of his strictly social documents. In Sub
Sole the emotion subsides although it does not disappear
completely. There are stories like "Eve of All Souls"
("Víspera de Difuntos"), in which pathos predominates
again drowning the frightening strangeness of the crime
that is narrated. The tone of tearful pathos diminishes.
The prose of Lillo acquires a resonance of angry protest
—in "Quilapán," for example— and attains a new di-
mension, more human and more abstract at the same
time, of regional and universal value in the unadorned
reproduction of a native custom, the cockfight in "In the
Cockpit" ("En la Rueda"), and in the elaboration of the
theme of divine malediction in "The Vagabond" ("El
Vagabundo"), the second version of "The Hand that
Stuck Fast" ("La Mano Pegada"). Lillo narrates these
sketches of everyday life in a conventional way. Nevertheless, in them you can see the search for the element of
surprise that can elevate the drama of the characters to
a plane of novelty genuinely artistic. Elements of this
kind are, for example, the death of the cock Clavel, the
decision of the captain in "The Towline" ("El Remolque"), the accident and the resurrection of the young
landowner in "The Vagabond" ("El Vagabundo"), and
the hair-raising vengeance of the shipwrecked man in
"The Drowned Man" ("El Ahogado") who drags along
with him his treasure.

In his narratives which are symbolic in character *Baldomero Lillo reaches a perfection that can be equalled only by the masters of the genre in Chile: Augusto D'Halmar and Pedro Prado. Traces of Darío are also evident here. Stories like "The Rape of the Sun" ("El Rapto del Sol"), a parable against ambition and pride; "Unredeemed" ("Irredención"), a type of story for children in which vanity is punished, and "Gold" ("El Oro") seem to have a direct relationship to the stories of Rubén Darío's Azul, not only because of the subject matter but also because of the style. On the other hand, "Eternal Snow" ("Las Nieves Eternas"), without doubt one of Lillo's masterpieces, differs from the poetic legends of Darío in the marvellous simplicity of the language and the really profound philosophy of the central idea. González Vera has pointed to a Spanish version of this tale,[14] in which the history of a drop of water is narrated, in a perfect cycle, from the time a ray of sunlight makes it fall from a mountain rock until a hurricane returns it—changed first into steam, then into snow—to the high mountains from which it started out. In this cycle, which is the cycle of life, man acquiesces and man refuses in the critical moments of love, in suffering, pity, pride, ambition and egotism. He searches for his destiny under divine inspiration. When he finds it, it is death he must face, in the cold, motionless perfection of eternal snow. Augusto D'Halmar imitated this story in his beautiful "Seeing the World" ("A Rodar Tierras").*

Let us say in passing that it is from Sub Sole that many tendencies emerge that carry great prestige in contemporary Chilean literature: stories about the sea, cultivated by Salvador Reyes, Juan Marín and Luis Enrique Délano, which have their origins in such stories as "The Towline" ("El Remolque"); stories demanding social justice for the Indian look back to "Quilapán"; the humorous

[14] It seems that it is influenced by a short story of Gregorio Martínez Sierra entitled "Travels of a Drop of Water" ("Viajes de una Gota de Agua"). Cf. González Vera, *op. cit.*, p. 238.

treatment of customs in the narrations of González Vera and Carlos León stems from "Inamible," which because of the technical perfection, the novelty and agility of its development and the rich imagination of the author is better than most of the stories in Sub Sole. It stands as one of the few really funny stories that Lillo wrote. The others are: "The Tip" ("La Propina"), "Shop and Back-room" ("Tienda y Trastienda") and "My Neighbors" ("Mis Vecinos"), which are included in Relatos Populares. To call stories like "The Hand that Stuck Fast" ("La Mano Pegada") and "Hunting Big Game" ("Caza Mayor") funny is an aberration. In these stories the pathos is overwhelming. "The Hand that Stuck Fast" is macabre in the scene in which the old vagabond suffers at the hands of the landlord. "The Shotgun" ("Cañuela y Petaca") is supposed to be funny, but it lacks the overflowing and contagious humor of "Inamible."

V.   Relatos Populares, 1942*

The stories of Baldomero Lillo included in this book did not appear in the two books he published during his lifetime, Sub Terra and Sub Sole. They were collected by González Vera from newspapers and reviews. In only one of these stories is the locale a mining camp, "The Abyss" ("Sobre el Abismo"). The rest cover a wide gamut of subjects: some of them are about contemporary customs like "In the Tenement House" ("En el Conventillo"), "Shop and Back-room" ("Tienda y Trastienda") and "My Neighbors" ("Mis Vecinos"); others are folk tales of the countryside like "Solomon's Cross" ("La Cruz de Salomón"), "The Little Angel" ("El Angelito"), "The Phantom with the Dishevelled Hair" ("La Chascuda") and "Marshmallow" ("Malvavisco"); others are dramas of the sea: "Sub-Sole," "The Whale" ("La Ballena"); and two are witty tales of the imagination: "The

* Tales of the People.

Tip" ("La Propina") and "Switchmen" ("Cambiadores"). Since this is a posthumous compilation you cannot expect to find in it the unity of Sub Terra. Nevertheless, in spite of the variety in the plots of the stories, there is something that characterizes all these stories. The indictment of society disappears, but not social awareness which is present in "The Little Angel" ("El Angelito") and "In the Tenement House" ("En el Conventillo"). Both these are charged with humanitarian fervor and indignation at the drama that drowns the social outcasts of both city and country. But all this suffering is contained. Lillo's desolate exclamatory tendency is controlled by a purifying force which is more than an artistic instinct; it is mastery, confidence, discerning power, a very broad vision. Relatos Populares is, like Sub Sole, perhaps even more so than Sub Sole, the creation of an experienced storyteller who is not satisfied with the immediate dramatic impact of the events that he puts naked before the reader, but who wants the reality that is hidden in the innermost recesses of the emotions, the passions, the weakness and grandeur of the soul of the people to have a more profound and permanent effect.

What is it but utter madness, that determination of the weavers who move into the wretched tenement house only to die of hunger, scorning charity, spitting on the hand of the person who dares to offer them aid and clinging to the bronze bedstead with their fingernails so that it may not be said that "one of the Mella 'girls' has died in the poor house"? On another plane, that of pure imagination and eccentricity of a high level, Lillo also gives his characters a touch of divine madness: that young man, for instance in "The Tip" ("La Propina") and his implacable executioner, the driver, who pursues him hanging on the tails of his coat while both run after the train. His predicament is absurd, but it is decisive, fatal, that is to say, classically tragic. From that race and the punches that he gives the driver —the weight of life— Octaviano Pioquinto obtains the secret of final redemption. And the young shopkeeper in "Shop and Back-room" ("Tienda y Trastienda"), who works without receiving wages, is also touched with this madness. So is his boss who has found a way of cheating everybody; so are the fat people who make drop curtains in "My Neighbors" ("Mis Vecinos"), who eat up the provisions of all the travelling salesmen and then disguise themselves to avoid paying; so is the strange passenger who has a premonition of the railroad catastrophe in "Switchmen" ("Cambiadores"). Those two fantasies "Sub-Sole" and "The Abyss" ("Sobre el Abismo"), Gothic tales of horror, the best that have been written in this genre, are certainly touched by madness. It has been said that "Sub-Sole" is an imitation of the short story "Alone!" ("¡Solo!") by Armando Palacio Valdés, but even if it were, the changes that Lillo introduces into the theme, the difference in characterization, the tension of his style which permits the highest drama and the subtlety of his poetry which never becomes exclamatory justify the name "master" bestowed on Lillo by the critics.

If we skip over "The Phantom with the Dishevelled Hair" ("La Chascuda"), a story in which the reasoning of the protagonist lacks solidity and the plot is poorly organized, and "The Whale" ("La Ballena"), a mood story but with no outcome, Relatos Populares proves that Baldomero Lillo reached a high level of technical perfection, of psychological depth and of imaginative force unequalled in the Chilean literature of his day. When his contemporaries are not able to avoid the commonplace in their eagerness to paint customs, Baldomero touches Chilean reality, he makes it palpitate with emotion, he animates it with a comic eccentricity, or he stylizes it in his search for higher values. What is obvious has no place in his conception of literature. He had already conquered the privilege of the sublime.

VI. El Hallazgo y Otros Cuentos del Mar, 1956.*

This is a compilation of three stories that Baldomero Lillo never published, which were discovered by the Chilean critic José Zamudio. Although they are uneven in quality, they do not change our opinion about the merits of Lillo. The first of the stories, entitled "The Discovery" ("El Hallazgo"), shows a curious resemblance, as Zamudio has observed, to Ernest Hemingway's novel The Old Man and the Sea. *In both these stories an old man sails out into the ocean to fight against forces ordained by fate to conquer him. But while in the work of Hemingway in the struggle the man comes to realize the basic heroic quality of his nature and attains an epic dignity in defeat, in the story of Lillo the heroism that the protagonist shows in his fight against other men is slight and the emotion at the end is of primitive drama. Lillo was not successful in breathing into his tale the universal quality that Hemingway gave to his. Nevertheless, three quarters of "The Discovery" ("El Hallazgo") possesses an austere grandeur and an emotional power always about to free themselves. For the student of Lillo there is in this story a curious detail: in the middle of the narrative he describes a whale hunt which is nothing less than a synthetic version of the story "The Whale" ("La Ballena") included in a previous volume,* Sub Sole.

The second story, "The Ring" ("El Anillo"), is semilegendary in character. If it had been treated as a magic tale, as the story demanded, without the natural explanation of the strange event that inspires it, its merit perhaps would be greater. It has the elements of a hairraising tale, but these elements are not used sufficiently. As for the third story, "The Dive" ("El Zambullón"), it does not inspire great feeling, perhaps owing to the fact that the effect of the shipwreck, which is imminent, is weakened because the reader is told that the shore is

---

* The Discovery and Other Tales of the Sea.

in swimming distance of the boat. The merit of the story rests on Theresa, a character of epic proportions, whom Lillo describes with vibrant feeling.

VII. The Timeliness of Lillo

With time Baldomero Lillo's prestige has become very solid, and today he is considered the father of social realism in Chilean literature. Nobody disputes his merits. Critics and writers of all tendencies analyze his writings in search of new aspects and new lessons. Everything that he wrote has been published. If other stories are discovered, they could possibly change appreciations that are strictly critical, but not the evaluation of his work as it is related to the development of Chilean literature.

Baldomero Lillo was not an isolated phenomenon of his day. Along with him there grew up a large group of novelists, short story writers, poets and essayists, whose work appears to us today to be solidly built upon principles which have already been recognized and defined by Chilean critics. These principles represent the crystallization of a Spanish American literary ideal fostered about the middle of the nineteenth century by such eminent thinkers as José Victorino Lastarria and Domingo Faustino Sarmiento. They responded to the cry to create a literature that would be truly Spanish American, something new, something valiant in its ideology which would be far from the trodden paths of classical and neoclassical European models. In a way they went beyond Spanish American romanticism since they came to inject into it the sap of French and Spanish realism, and the modernista exoticism of Rubén Darío. The reform of Darío, which affected verse as well as prose, was received by the Chilean writers of 1900 without a clear idea of its significance. Its more superficial side did not interest them. They were writers preoccupied with a social ideal, with philosophical and political credos, and therefore scornful of vain rhetorical acrobatics. Nevertheless, they

*were attracted by the literary allegory which the moder-
nista writers imported from the Orient.*

*From this duality, French and Spanish realism on
the one hand and oriental idealism on the other, there
was born in Chile and in other Spanish American coun-
tries a hybrid literature which never was able to reconcile
the extremes of the tendencies which animated it. This
phenomenon explains how Baldomero Lillo was able to
write the naturalistic short stories of* Sub Terra *and the
philosophical allegories of* Sub Sole, *and it also explains
how Augusto D'Halmar could write* Juana Lucero *alongside* The Lamp in the Mill (La Lámpara en el Molino);
Pedro Prado, Alsino *alongside* A Rural Judge (Un Juez
Rural); *and Eduardo Barrios,* Perdition (Un Perdido)
alongside Brother Ass (El Hermano Asno).

*What fundamentally differentiates Baldomero Lillo
from the other writers of his generation if they all have
a common literary ancestry? A fact that might explain
his timeliness: the powerful and obsessive social preoccu-
pation of his writing. Neither D'Halmar, Latorre, Santiván, Maluenda, Prado, nor Barrios showed this desire to
create in their books the climate of burning social conflict
that Lillo pursued blindly throughout his stories. Nevertheless, it would be wrong to consider him a political
writer. He was not one. But he was a revolutionary writer,
profoundly and genuinely revolutionary, because of the
dynamic quality he injected in his stories about poor
people and because, without ever falling into discursive
propaganda, his stories always contain an implicit mo-
rality which is a call for social justice, a call to come to
the defense of the poor and the helpless. As has already
been said, although his ideology is Christian, his characters, his themes, all the world that he brought to life in
his literary production show the roots of modern Socialism.*

*The message of Baldomero Lillo has found an echo
in the work of recent authors: in many of the short stories
of Manuel Rojas, in the dry humor of González Vera's*

narratives; *Juan Marín followed him in his novel* Black
Wind (Viento Negro), *which brought up to date the
drama of the coal mines; young writers like Nicomedes
Guzmán, Gonzalo Drago, Baltasar Castro and others
study him, praise him, make a cult of him, always trying
to emulate him in novels and short stories of crude
realism.*

   *To sum up, it can be said that Baldomero Lillo cre-
ated a literary tradition in Chile: a tradition of realism
in the description of the social problems of the proletari-
at and, like the other writers of his generation, he sought
a form to express his conception of life in allegorical
idealism. In both directions he created works of universal
significance which assure for him a seat of honor among
the great short story writers of Spanish America.*

Fernando Alegría
University of California, Berkeley
January, 1958

TABLE OF SOURCES *

From *Sub Terra; Cuadros Mineros*. Santiago de Chile, Imprenta Moderna, 1904. 221 p. (and subsequent editions):

> Gate No. 12
> Firedamp
> Pay Day
> The Devil's Pit
> The Well
> Juan Fariña (Legend)
> The Drill
> The Shotgun

From *Sub Sole*. Santiago de Chile, Imprenta y Encuadernación Universitaria, 1907. 181 p. (and subsequent editions):

> The Towline
> *Inamible*
> The Trap

From *Relatos Populares*. Preface, selection and bibliography by J. S. González Vera. Santiago de Chile, Editorial Nascimento, 1942, 234 p.:

> Sub-Sole
> In the Tenement House
> The Abyss

---

* The stories listed were translated by Dr. Esther S. Dillon, with the exception of "Pay Day," "The Devil's Pit," and "*Inamible.*" These three were translated by Professor Angel Flores and revised by Dr. Esther S. Dillon.

TABLE OF CONTENTS

GATE No. 12

Pablo clung instinctively to his father's legs. His ears buzzed and the floor sped downward beneath his feet giving him a strange sensation of anguish. He felt as though he were being hurled into that black hole he had glimpsed as he entered the cage. His large, round eyes looked fearfully on the dark walls of the shaft down which they were descending with dizzying rapidity. In that silent descent, without a sound save the dripping of water on the iron top, the lamplights seemed about to go out, and in their feeble rays could be vaguely distinguished, on the uneven shaft wall, a whole interminable series of black shadows that shot upwards like arrows.

In a minute, the speed diminished abruptly; his feet felt solid again on that fugitive floor and the heavy iron cage, with a harsh rasping of chains and hinges, stood still at the entrance to the haulageway.

The old man took the little boy's hand and together they entered the dark passageway. They were among the first arrivals. Work in the mine had not yet begun. Of the haulageway, which was high enough to allow the miner to stand at full height, all that could be seen was a part of the roof above, crossed by great thick beams. The side walls were invisible in the profound darkness that filled the vast, gloomy excavation.

Forty yards from the digging area, they stopped before a kind of grotto hollowed out of the rock. From the cracked, sooty roof hung a tin lantern whose weak beam of light gave the room the appearance of a crypt, draped in black and peopled with shadows. A little old man sat behind a table at the back writing in an enormous ledger. His black suit made a sharp contrast to his pale, deeply wrinkled face. At the sound of footsteps he raised his head and fixed a questioning glance on the old miner who, advancing timidly, in a submissive and respectful voice said:

"Sir, I've brought the boy."

With one sweep, the foreman's penetrating eyes took in the weak little body of the boy. His delicate limbs and the childish ingenuity of the dark face with its wide-open shining eyes, like those of a frightened little animal, impressed the foreman unfavorably. In spite of a heart hardened to the daily spectacle of so much misery, he felt a pitying uneasiness at the sight of that little fellow, yanked from his childish games to be condemned, like so many others, to languish miserably in damp passageways, next to the ventilation doors. The hard lines of his face softened and with assumed severity he adressed the old man who anxiously awaited his reply:

"Heavens, man, this child is too weak to work. Is he your son?"

"Yes, sir."

"Well, you should have pity on his youth and rather than bury him in here, you should be sending him to school for a while."

"But, sir," stammered the shaky, supplicating voice of the miner, "there are six of us at home and only one working. Pablo is eight already and he should earn the bread he eats. As a miner's son, he'll have to be a miner, too, and there's no other school for that but the mine."

A sudden coughing attack drowned out his trembling voice, but his moist eyes implored with such insistence that the foreman, won over by that mute appeal, raised a whistle to his lips. Its piercing sound echoed down the deserted passageway. Hurried steps were heard and a dark silhouette appeared in the doorway.

"Juan," exclaimed the little man, pointing to the miner's son, "take this boy to Gate No. 12. He will replace José, the hauler's son, who was run over yesterday."

Then, turning to the old miner, who was about to murmur his thanks, he said severely, "I've noticed that in the last week you haven't reached the five car minimum for every digger. Don't forget that if it happens again you'll have to be laid off and a more active man put in your place," and with an energetic gesture, he dismissed him.

The three walked silently along and the sound of their footsteps gradually grew faint in the obscure tunnel. They walked between two rails. The unevenly spaced ties, sunken into the muddy floor, tripped them up constantly. They guided themselves by the spikes which held the ties to the rails. The guide, still a young man, went on ahead, while the old miner, his head sunken on his chest, followed dragging Pablo by the hand. The foreman's warning had filled the old man's heart with desolation. For some time it had been apparent to all that he was losing ground. Each day he drew nearer to that fatal limit which, once passed, turns an old worker into a worthless hindrance in the mine.

From dawn to dark, for fourteen long hours, coiled up like a serpent, he furiously attacked the coal, picking at the unending lode that so many generations of miserable men like him had scratched at ceaselessly in the entrails of the earth.

But the tenacious, unyielding struggle soon turned even the most vigorous young ones into decrepit old men. There in that damp, narrow hole, their backs hunched and their muscles grew weak. Like the recalcitrant colt who trembles at the sight of the whip, these old miners felt their tired flesh quiver as they returned to their digging each day. But hunger is more effective than the whip or the spur. So they silently went on with their overwhelming task. The whole vein, eaten away in a thousand places by that human borer, vibrated and let go piece by piece, bitten by the tooth of the pick, just as the sandy shore gives way to the onrushing sea.

The guide stopped, suddenly ending the old man's sad meditations. A door shut off their path in that direction. On the floor, up against the wall, barely discernible in the flickering light of the lamps was a small, vaguely outlined, huddled shape: it was a ten year old boy crouched in the hollow of the wall.

With his elbows on his knees and his pale face between his hands, silent and motionless, he seemed not even to see the workers who passed the threshold and then left him again in the darkness. His open, expressionless eyes were fixed dreamily on high, absorbed, perhaps, in the contemplation of some imaginary panorama which, like a desert mirage, attracted his eyes, thirsty for light, wet with nostalgia for the distant day's splendor. He had charge of the door, and he spent the interminable hours of his interment submerged in a sad self-absorption, weighted down by that enormous sepulchral stone that crushed in him forever all the restless and graceful mobility of childhood. It is the suffering of these children that leaves, in the souls of those who understand them, infinite bitterness and resentment against the execrable crime committed by human egoism and cowardice.

After traveling along a narrow manway, the two men and the boy finally came out into the upper level haulageway, from the roof of which continuously fell great drops of water. From time to time, there could be heard a muted distant roar, like that of a gigantic hammer pounding the earth's crust. Although Pablo did not know it, that sound was made by the shock of the waves hitting the rocky shore. A short walk brought them to Gate No. 12.

"This is it," said the guide, stopping before a door that swung from a wooden frame fitted into the rock. So thick were the shadows that the reddish glow of their lamps scarcely showed up the obstacle before them.

Pablo, who failed to understand the reason for their stopping, looked silently at his companions, who, after a rapid, short interchange, began cheerfully to show him how to operate the door. Following their directions, the boy opened and shut it several times, dispelling all his father's fears that he would lack the necessary strength for such a task.

The old man showed his approval by caressing with his calloused hand the tousled head of his first-born who still showed no fatigue or fear. His youthful imagination was impressed by the new scenes. It seemed as though he were in a dark room and he expected at any moment that a window would be opened to let in the bright rays of the sun. Although his inexperienced little heart no longer suffered the fright that the descent in the shaft had produced, his suspicious fears were now aroused by the unusual demonstrations of affection from his father.

A light shone in the distance. The squeaking of wheels on the tracks and a heavy pounding of hooves resounded on the floor.

"It's the car!" both men exclaimed. "Quick, Pablo," said his father, "let's see if you can do your job."

Fists clenched, Pablo pushed his tiny body against the door until it touched the wall. Just in time. Then a dark, sweating, panting horse trotted by pulling a heavy carload of coal.

The miners exchanged an approving glance. Pablo was now an experienced gate boy. The old man bent over him, and in flattering tones told him that now he was a big boy, not like those cry-babies up above that clung to their mother's skirts. He was a real man now, a worker, a fellow comrade who would be treated as such. And in few words he made him understand that he would have to stay by himself. He mustn't be afraid. There were lots of boys like him in the mine doing the same work. He was near and would come to see him from time to time. When the day's work was done, they would go home together.

Pablo listened with increasing fright. His only answer was to clutch his father's smock with both hands.
Up to then, he had not fully comprehended what they
wanted of him. The unexpected turn that this innocent
little excursion had taken filled him with horror. He must
get out of this place. He wanted to see his mother and
his brothers and sisters, to be out in the daylight again.
All his father's persuasion brought forth only the cry:

"Let's go home!"

Promises, menaces, nothing availed. He could only
wail in mounting and unbearable fear:

"Let's go home, Daddy!"

At first, the old miner's face showed violent annoyance, but when he saw turned up to him those desolate,
supplicating, tear-filled eyes, his rising anger changed to
infinite pity—he was so small and weak! The paternal love
so long suppressed in him suddenly flooded his whole
being.

The memory of his own life —forty years of work
and suffering— suddenly stood out clearly before him.
He had to admit with regret that all that was left of that
immense labor was an exhausted body that would soon
be relegated to the waste pile. That this child awaited
a similar destiny in the mine made him want desperately
to deny a victim to this insatiable monster that dragged
scarcely grown children from their mothers' laps to con-
vert them into pariahs whose bent backs received with
equal stoicism the brutal lash of the master and the scraping caresses of the rock in the narrow, sloping tunnels.

But the spark of rebellion in him was quickly extinguished by the remembered picture of his poor home and
hungry, unclad beings for whom he was the only pro-
vider. His own experience taught him that his dream was
foolish. The mine never freed those whom it had caught.
Like new links that substituted for the old broken down
ones in the endless chain down there, sons succeeded
fathers. In the deep pit the rising and descending of the
human tide never ceased. The young ones, breathing the

poisoned air, grew up with rickets, weak and pale. But they had to resign themselves, for to this they had been born.

So, with a determined gesture, the old man undid from his waist a strong, narrow cord. In spite of the child's struggles and protests, he fastened it about Pablo's waist. Then he attached the other end to a bolt in the wall. Old pieces of cord hanging there indicated that this was not the first time it had served such a purpose.

The child, frightened to death, let out penetrating shrieks of awful anguish and they had to drag him forcibly from between his father's legs, which he grasped with all his strength. His pleadings and cries filled the tunnel. The tender victim, even more unfortunate than the biblical Isaac, heard not a single friendly voice that would deter the paternal hand turned against his own flesh because of the crime and the iniquity of men.

His cries calling the departing old man were so heart-rending, piercing and vibrant that the poor father felt his resolve weakening again. But that only lasted a minute. Covering his ears, so as not to hear the shrieks that tore his heart, he hastened his step to get away from the place. Before leaving the haulageway, he stopped and listened. A little voice, weakened by the distance, cried from afar, "Mama! Mama!"

Then, the father ran like a crazy man chased by the wailing cry and he never stopped until he reached the vein. At the sight of it, his grief turned to fury and grabbing his pick he attacked it madly. His blows hit the block like heavy hail on resounding glass. The steel pick buried itself in that shiny black mass knocking out enormous pieces that fell in a pile about the miner's feet, while a thick veil of dust covered the flickering light of his lamp. The sharp fragments flew all about him, cutting his face, neck and bare chest. Streams of blood mixed with the copious perspiration that ran down his wet body that was like a wedge in the opened breach. He pushed against it with the frenzy of a prisoner who bores through the wall that closes him in. But he had none of the hope that gives strength to the prisoner who may find at the end of *his* task a new life full of sun, air and freedom.

FIREDAMP

In the shaft all movement had come to a standstill. The unloaders sat smoking silently between the rows of empty cars. The overseer, a thin little man, whose shaven face with its high cheekbones revealed firmness and astuteness, stood waiting motionless, with his lantern lit, next to the stopped elevator. Above them, the sun shone in a cloudless sky and a light breeze from the coast brought with it in invisible waves the salty tang of the ocean.

Suddenly, at the door of the shaft house appeared the mine inspector. As he came forward his footsteps rang out on the iron platform. He wore a raincoat and carried a lantern in his left hand. Without even bothering to answer the timid greeting of the overseer, he entered the cage, followed by his subordinate. A second later they disappeared silently into the dark abyss.

Two minutes later, when the elevator stopped at the main entry, the bursts of laughter, the voices and the shouts which usually echoed through that part of the mine, ceased as if by magic. A fearful whispering rose from the shadows and extended quickly under the black vaults.

Mister Davis, the chief inspector, was somewhat fat, but very tall and strong with a red face on which whiskey had stamped its seal. He inspired the miners with an almost superstitious fear and respect. Hard and inflexible, in his treatment of the miners he knew no pity. In the pride of his race, he considered the lives of these beings unworthy the attention of a gentleman. But that same gentleman would roar with fury if his horse or his dog were the victims of the slightest neglect in the care that their precious lives demanded.

The most timid protest on the part of these poor devils infuriated him as though it were a rebellion. He believed that their animal-like passivity was right, that any deviation from it deserved severe punishment.

The tours which his job as mine inspector required of him from time to time were the bane of his refined and sybaritic existence. A devilish humor possessed him during those wearisome visits. His irritability spent itself on punishments and fines which fell indiscriminately on great and small. His presence in the mine —announced by the white light of his lantern— was more feared than cave-ins or explosions.

That day, as always, the news of his coming had produced a certain nervous excitement in all sections of the mine. The miners cast suspicious eyes on every little light that shone in the shadows, expecting to see at any minute that dreaded white ray. Everywhere the work proceeded with feverish activity; the diggers, their bodies bent over in impossible positions, hacked out the brittle mineral piece by piece and the loaders pushed their creaking cars down the haulageways.

The inspector, with his companion, stopped for a few moments in the foremen's office where he informed himself of the details and needs which had made his presence necessary. After giving a few orders, still accompanied by the overseer, he headed for the interior of the mine through winding levels and narrow, mud-filled passageways.

Seated on the bottom of a car from which the sides had been removed, he from time to time made some observation to the overseer, who with great difficulty followed behind. Two boys, clad in nothing but cloth trousers, moved this unusual vehicle. One pushed from behind and the other, hitched like a horse, pulled in front. The latter showed serious signs of fatigue: his body bathed in perspiration and the anguished expression on his face revealed the exhaustion of excessive muscular effort. A kind of leather harness pressed against his bare chest and from the belt around his waist ran two ropes which were tied to the front of the car.

At the entrance to a level which led to the new workings, the inspector, whose attention was fixed on the roof timbers, called a halt. Directing the beam of his lantern upward, he began to examine the seepage through the rock, poking with a thin iron rod the timbers which held up the roof. Some of these had menacing curves and the rod went through them as though they were some bland, spongy thing. The overseer anxiously looked on in silent foreboding. He felt already one of those storms that so often crashed about his head, in his position as a humble and servile subordinate.

"Come over here. How long ago was this collar timbered?"

"About a month ago, sir," answered the troubled overseer.

"A month —and the timbers are already rotted. You're stupid! You let yourself be fooled by the timberers who put white wood in saturated places like this. You'll see to it right now that this is remedied before your negligence catches up with you!"

The terrified overseer withdrew hastily and disappeared into the darkness.

Mister Davis prodded with his rod the bare back of the boy who was in front and the car moved, but slowly, because the slope made the pulling painful on that slippery, soft floor. The one in back helped his younger companion with all his strength, but suddenly the wheels refused to budge and the car stopped. The young lead boy lay face down in the mud, both hands still on the rails in pulling position. In spite of his courage, exhaustion had taken its toll.

The angry voice of the inspector rang out through

the tunnel. He was beside himself at the prospect of having to drag himself, doubled in two, over those dirty wet puddles.

"You blithering idiot! Slacker!" he shrieked in a fury.

The boy dragged himself up on his knees and, making a supreme effort, stood up. There was in his eyes a look of rage, pain and despair. With a nervous movement, he threw off those beast-of-burden trappings and leaned against the wall, where he remained motionless.

Mister Davis, who didn't miss a move, got off the car and approached him with his rod held high, saying:

"Oh, so you resist, eh? Just wait..."

But seeing that the victim's only defense were the arms that he held crossed above his head, he stopped, hesitated a moment, and then, in a thundering voice shouted:

"Get going! Get out of here!"

Turning to the other boy, who was trembling like a leaf, he ordered imperiously:

"You —follow me!"

And all doubled over, he headed down the dark tunnel.

After having dispatched a group of repairmen to reinforce the timbers, the overseer had gone to wait for his chief in an open space that adjoined the new working areas. To his astonishment, after a long while the inspector appeared with a very red face, breathing heavily and spattered with mud from head to foot. So great was the overseer's surprise, that he didn't even move toward the inspector, who, letting himself down heavily on some timbers, began to shake his clothes and to wipe away with his fine handkerchief the beads of perspiration that ran down his face.

The boy who came up pushing the small car told the overseer briefly what had happened. He listened to the news with trepidation; then, assuming the most alarmed and tragic expression he could muster, he solicitously approached the inspector. The latter, realizing that the whole incident would hurt his pride, had recovered his usual haughty and supremely disdainful attitude. Fixing on the servile face of his subordinate the cold, implacable stare of his gray eyes, he askd with a voice that hid a certain controlled irritation:

"Does that boy have any relatives?"

"He only has a mother and three small brothers. His father died, crushed in a cave-in, when they began the new workings. He was a good miner," added the overseer trying to minimize the faults of the son with the good qualities of the father.

"Well, you will order immediately that that woman and her children vacate their house. I won't have slackers here," he ended with increasing severity.

His tone admitted no reply. The overseer, with one knee on the wet ground, wrote a few lines in his notebook by the light of his lamp. While he wrote, his imagination transferred him to the home of that poor widow and her orphans. Accustomed as he was to these evictions, in his role as executor of the owner's implacable justice, even he could not help feeling a certain distaste for this measure that would bring ruin to that miserable hovel.

His scribbling finished, he tore out the sheet and calling the boy to him, he said:

"Take this outside to the housing manager."

The inspector and the overseer were now alone. In this space, which served as a materials deposit, by the light of the lantern could be seen reinforcement timbers, heaps of rails and pick handles scattered about along the walls where here and there blacker spots marked the openings to sinister manways.

From these holes, in short and intermittent vibrations, came the sound as of faraway breaking waves. The squeaking of wheels, the babble of human voices, dry crackling noises and a slow drumming, impossible to localize, filled the massive vault of that deep cavern.

Here the black shadows limited the circle of light to the smallest radius; against it their compact masses lay in constant ambush, ready always to advance or recede.

Suddenly, in the distance, there appeared a light, followed by another, then another, on and on. They seemed like small balloons floating on a sea of ink that rose and fell following the undulating curve of an invisible tide.

The overseer took out his watch and interrupted the embarrassing silence:

"These are the diggers from Media Hoja. They are coming to talk about the special allowances. Yesterday they made the plan to discuss in here." And he went on elaborating the minute details of the matter, to which his superior listened with obvious displeasure. He frowned, everything about him revealed a growing impatience and when the overseer began to repeat his arguments:

"It is therefore impossible to raise the allowance because then the price of coal...," a dry and harsh "I already know that" cut him off abruptly.

The overseer cast a furtive glance at his interrupter and, in the darkness, a scarcely perceptible, skeptical smile played over his lips as he noticed the long line of approaching lights. It was easy to see that the business of these poor devils ran the grave risk of turning into a disaster. He was more than ever convinced of this when he saw the inspector's frown and the state to which the journey through the mine had reduced his person and clothes.

The knees of his trousers showed great splotches of mud. His hands, usually so white and well cared for, were those of a miner. He had doubtlessly tripped and fallen more than once. Besides, the stains on his crushed hat, from the soot that the lamps deposit on the tunnel roofs, indicated that his head had really tested how hard and solid were those timbers that he had before found so fragile! As the overseer continued his observations, a malignant joy lit up his astute face. He felt, at least in part, avenged for the daily humiliations he had to suffer.

The lights gradually drew near and there could be heard, distinctly now, the sound of voices and the splashing of feet in the liquid mud. The head of the column reached the storage area. The men lined up silently, facing their superiors. The lampsmoke and the acrid odor of sweating bodies soon impregnated the air with a nauseating and asphyxiating stench. In spite of the considerable increase in light, the shadows still persisted. In them were sketched the blurred silhouettes of the miners, like confused masses of indeterminate and vague outline.

Mr. Davis sat impassive on his bench, hands crossed on his fat paunch, the strong contours of his powerful muscles barely visible in the gloomy light.

The sepulchral silence was suddenly broken by the hollow, hacking cough of an old man. The inspector raised his lantern head high and projected its luminous rays on the miners. Cap in hand, a man detached himself from the group and stopped three paces away.

He was short, sunken-chested, with angular shoulders. His bald head, blackened as was his face over which hung long wisps of gray hair, gave him a ludicrous and grotesque appearance. A knowing glance from the overseer gave him courage. In a trembling voice, he stated the problem that had brought them there. It was quite simple:

As the new vein was only sixty centimetres thick, they had to excavate four decimetres more of hard tuff in order to make room for the cars. This was the hardest work of all because the tuff was very solid. The presence of firedamp prohibited the use of explosives. They had to deepen the cut with their picks, all of which took considerable time and effort. The small raise in price per car, fixed at thirty centavos, was not sufficient since, although they began at dawn and didn't leave the mine until nighttime, they could scarcely fill three cars. Those who could raise that number to four were so few that they could be counted on the fingers of one hand. After painting a serious picture of the misery of their homes and the hunger of their wives and children, he ended up saying that only the hope of the allowance, promised when they took on the job in the new vein, had kept him and his companions going during the last two weeks.

There followed a lugubrious silence broken only by the light hissing of the lamps and an occasional chronic cough. Suddenly, the whole group stirred, heads were raised and everyone listened. The inspector's questioning voice sounded out:

"How much allowance do you want per metre?"

That concrete and final question received no answer. A murmur from the lines and some isolated voices could be heard, but they were silenced immediately when the imperious voice bitterly rang out:

"What's the matter? No answer?"

The old man, shifting his hat indecisively from one hand to the other, questioned thus directly, took a step forward. Trying to see in the hidden face of his interlocutor the effect of his words, in a slow, insecure voice he answered:

"Sir, the just thing would be that we be paid the price of four cars for each metre, because..."

He didn't finish. The engineer had risen and his obese figure stood out with menacing proportions in the shadowy darkness.

"You're a bunch of insolent imbeciles," he shrieked, his voice boiling over with anger, "to think that I am going to throw away the company's money to foster the laziness of a bunch of slackers who, instead of working, go to sleep like pigs in the corners of the mine!"

There was a pause as he took a deep breath, then he added, as if to himself:

"But I know all your tricks and take the hypocritical complaints of such trash for what they are worth."

Then, emphasizing each word, he turned to the overseer and ordered:

"You will pay an allowance of thirty centavos per metre of tuff to those who mine a minimum of four cars of coal a day. Those that do not reach that number will receive only the price of the coal."

He was furious because, in spite of all attempted economies, the coal from that vein was costing more than that of the other sections. The demands of the miners, which made the failure of the whole project more obvious, only served to increase his anger.

Under their black masks the miners' faces turned livid. Those words vibrated in their ears, echoing in the depths of their souls like the apocalyptic trumpeting of Judgment Day. Their eyes reflected a stupid, almost idiotic expression; their knees weakened as though suddenly the whole shadowy mine vault had come down upon them.

But so great was the fear that this irritated and imposing figure inspired in them and so powerful the domination that this unquestioned authority exercised over these poor spirits —weakened by so many years of slavery— that no one made a gesture nor let escape a single protest.

But later the reaction set in. The deprivation was so enormous, the punishment so severe, that for an instant their brains had been stunned by the blow, but they soon recovered. The first to come to his senses was the old man with the blackened bald head. Seeing that the inspector was about to leave, he stood resolutely in his way, pleading:

"Sir, be merciful! Have pity on us! Make them keep their promise, we beg you on our knees!"

But the inspector didn't even hear him. He was too busy discussing with the overseer the new tunnel which was to join the old diggings to the new.

A menacing murmur arose behind him as he started off. When the old man saw that he was leaving, he grabbed him by the sleeve. In the obscurity, a formidable arm rose and with a furious blow landed the daring miner three paces away. A muted thud, a moan —then all was silent. A moment later the inspector and the overseer disappeared around a corner.

Then there ensued a scene worthy of the souls condemned to Hell. In the blackness of the shadows the lamplights moved to and fro in all directions. Terrible curses and atrocious blasphemies resounded in the darkness and echoed sadly down the walls of rock which were as insensible as human egoism to their immense desolation.

Some had thrown themselves down on the floor where, like mute, inert masses, they lay completely oblivious, neither seeing nor hearing what went on about them. One old man wept silently and the tears ran down the deep furrows of the coppery, wrinkled skin of his blackened face. In other groups heated discussions, with much gesticulation, were going on while curses and roars of anger and disappointment interrupted the noise of the dispute. One tall, skinny boy, his fists tightly clenched, went from one group to another listening to the different opinions. Finally convinced that there was no remedy, that the sentence imposed was without appeal, in a fit of fury he hurled his lamp against the wall where it shattered into a thousand pieces.

Little by little they quieted down. One big, strong, young man exclaimed:

"I'll not dig one more piece of coal —to hell with it!"

"That's easy to say when you haven't got a wife and children," was someone's prompt reply.

"If we could only use powder —that damned firedamp!" complained the old baldhead.

"Oh, that wouldn't make any difference. As soon as they saw we were making a little more, they'd lower the pay."

"And you young ones are to blame," piped up one old man.

"Come now, gramps, hold your horses," spoke up the strong, young miner.

"O yes!" insisted the old man, "you and no one but you are to blame. You work so hard the rest of us can't keep up with you. If you'd ease up, prices wouldn't go down and this dog's life wouldn't be so hard to take."

"It's just that we don't like to loaf."

"Well, I've never loafed and you can see how well I've done!"

They all lapsed once more into silence. An old man who had been moaning in a corner rose and slowly left. Very soon the rest followed his example and in the depths of the gangway the vacillating lights were again submerged in those tenebrous waves that engulfed in an instant their fugitive, dying radiance.

* * *

On the new level the excavation work had been interrupted momentarily and only the repairmen were there: three men and a boy. Two were busy sawing the timbers and the other two were putting them into place. They were finishing up now and only a few yards separated them from the rock wall which was being opened up. A workman and the boy were trying to set up a vertical timber. The man held it while the boy with a sledge hammer hit heavy blows high on the timber. But since they were getting nowhere, they decided to take it out and shorten it. But the timber was stuck so solidly that, in spite of all their efforts, they could not budge it. Then they began to blame each other bitterly for the faulty measurement. After a sharp exchange, they separated and each sat down to rest on the rock-strewn floor.

One of the workmen who had been sawing came over, examined the upright, and seeing the hammer marks high on the timber near the ceiling, he said to the boy:

"You watch out. Don't hit it so high. One spark, just one, and we'll all be blown to bits in this hell. Come over here, come see," he added, squatting at the foot of the wall.

"Put your hand here. What do you feel?"

"Something like a little breeze blowing."

"Breeze —nothing, my friend. That's firedamp. Yesterday we covered several cracks with clay but this one must have escaped us. The whole airway must be filled with the damned gas."

And to make sure, he lifted the safety lamp high over his head. The flame reached out growing considerably longer. His arm came down in a hurry!

"The devil," he said, "there's enough firedamp here to blow up the whole mine!"

The boy, about eighteen or nineteen years old, was known by the unusual nickname of Black Wind. He was very dark, with strong, sinewy muscles and his pockmarked face showed a firmness and resolution that contrasted sharply with the timid and expressionless faces of his companions.

The miner and the boy continued their conversation seated on a timber:

"You see," said the former, "we are, worse luck, right inside the barrel of a shotgun in the place where the charge is put," and pointing out before him the high passageway, he continued:

"At the slightest carelessness, should a spark fly or a lamp break —the Devil pulls the trigger and out comes the shot. As for those of us who are here, we would simply be the dead partridges."

Black Wind did not answer. Down the airway he saw the inspector's lantern. The other workman had also seen it and both hastily leaped to their interrupted task. The boy began to hammer again but his companion stopped him.

"Don't you see, stupid, that it's useless?"

"But there they come and we have to do something."

"I'll do nothing and when they get here I'll tell them to give me another assistant, because you just won't listen to me."

So the argument started all over again. They would

have come to blows had not the arrival of their superiors interrupted them.

The inspector and the overseer examined the reinforcements carefully. Immediately the keen eye of the overseer lit upon the timber that had caused the fight.

"What's this, Juan?" he asked.

"It's his fault," answered the workman pointing to the boy. "He does what he wants and won't obey orders."

The overseer's penetrating eyes fixed themselves on Black Wind and suddenly he exclaimed:

"Why, you're the one who cut the signal wire in the foremen's office yesterday. That will cost you a five-peso fine for your little trick."

"I didn't do it!" roared the boy, pale with anger.

The overseer shrugged indifferently. Then, noticing the boy's furious look, he screamed imperiously:

"What are you doing, you damned loafer? Get that upright out, right now!"

The boy stood absolutely still. The unjust fine lashed his wild and rebellious soul and drove his fiery, strong character to its limit.

The overseer, infuriated by this defiance of his authority, grabbed him by the collar, pushed him forward and added insult to injury wth a violent kick. He had gone too far! Black Wind turned on him like a tiger, charged head first, hit him full force on the solar plexus and stretched him out cold on the floor.

At the sound of the thud, the inspector, who had been taking down notes, turned to interfere. As he did, he saw a dark shadow slipping along the wall. With a leap he stood in its path. The fugitive tried to slip by but an iron fist grabbed his arm and dragged him back.

Having regained consciousness, the overseer, breathing heavily, sat on a stone surrounded by the workmen. When he haw his aggressor, he wanted to go for him but a sign from the inspector stopped him.

"He butted him," explained the workmen.

Without letting go his prisoner, the inspector dragged him to the upright. His tone was quiet, almost friendly:

"Before you do anything else, you're going to put that timber in place."

"I've said I don't want to work."

"I say you shall work and if the hammer isn't enough, try your head, you're so good at using that."

At the burst of laughter that followed this sally, the boy's disfigured face turned livid with rage. He looked around like a caged beast and in his eyes was the dark flame of an unswerving resolve. Suddenly, contracting his muscles, he jumped, trying to escape between the engineer and the wall. A terrible punch that caught him head on knocked him flat on his back. He got up on his hands and knees, but a furious kick in the kidneys sent him rolling on the debris. The men watched avidly with bated breath.

Black Wind, horrible looking, full of mud and all bloody, got to his feet. A stream of blood spouted from his right eye and ran down to the corners of his mouth, but with a firm step he went forward. Grabbing the sledge hammer, he hit the leaning timber with furious blows.

A smirk of satisfied pride lighted up the engineer's fat face. He had tamed the wild beast. At each blow he repeated:

"Fine, boy, fine —bravo!"

Only the overseer saw the peril but he just managed to get to his feet. One after another in the blackness overhead shone great sparks. Black Wind had let the handle slip down through his hands to the very end and the steel as it struck full force against the sharp edges of the rock, like a great flint, produced the flaring sparks.

A blue flame shot down the curved collar of the tunnel and the mass of air within its walls ignited in a tremendous blaze. Just one brief second of that vision —then a powerful explosion tore at the bowels of the earth. Enveloped in a whirlwind of flames, stones and cracked beams, the six men were blown down the whole length of the tunnel.

At the sound of the formidable explosion, the inhabitants above rushed to their windows and doors where before their amazed eyes the mine structures erupted like a veritable volcano.

Beneath the serene blue sky, where not a trace of smoke nor flame was visible, the beams of the tipple, yanked as though by some prodigious force, suddenly flew skyward in all directions. One of the steel cages, traveling upward in the shaft, like a ball out of a cannon, shot straight up into the air to a tremendous height. There was a mad rush of women and children to the mine. Chaos everywhere. Workmen ran about aimlessly, terrified, not knowing what to do. But the presence of mind of the overseer on duty calmed them down somewhat. Under his direction, they set to work with feverish activity. The cages had disappeared, and with them, one of the cables, but the other cable was still intact, wound up on its drum. A pulley was hurriedly set over the shaft, a wooden bucket tied to the end of the cable, and all was set to go down. Just as the overseer and two workmen were about to get started, a great puff of thick smoke stopped them. They would have to wait for the ventilators to clear the air.

Meanwhile the crazed wives of the trapped miners had invaded the platform, greatly impeding rescue operations. In order to clear their working space, the men had to fight them off, and their screaming made it difficult to hear the orders of the foremen and engineers.

Finally, the smoke cleared away and the workers got into the wooden bucket. The down signal was given and they disappeared in the midst of profound silence.

At the entrance to the haulageway they left the improvised cage and went inside. It was deathly quiet and as black as night. The whole place was swept clean of obstacles. Not a sign of timbers nor cars. Pulleys, cables, signal cords, beams —all had been blown to smithereens in the explosion. Only one thought was uppermost in the rescuers' minds: were all their comrades dead?

Soon a great number of lights appeared and they found themselves surrounded by workers. On hearing the rumblings they had headed for the exit as fast as their feet would carry them, but out in the central haulageway they were brought to a halt by the smoke and poisonous air. They could only guess about what had happened to the workers at the entrance; ninety-nine chances out of a hundred, they were buried under the rubble at the bottom of the shaft.

They agreed that the explosion must have taken place in the new level and that the timberers, the inspector and head overseer must have perished.

A unanimous shout —"Let's go!"— rang out and they all started to move but the energetic voice of the overseer stopped them:

"No one is to move," he said authoritatively. "This place is reeking with blackdamp. The first thing we'll have to do is get the ventilators going. Shut the gates of the second airways so that the air can work directly into the haulageway. Then we'll see what we can do."

While everyone ran to carry out the orders, Tomás, a tall strong lad, came over and said resolutely:

"I'll go if there is someone who will come with me. It's cowardly to just leave them there like that. They might still be alive."

"Yes, yes, let's go," shouted twenty or more voices.

The overseer tried to dissuade them, saying they were going to an almost certain death. The explosion had ocurred more than two hours before, so there was no chance at all that any of them might have survived. But, seeing that the men would not listen to him, he finally gave in. They all wanted to be in the rescue party, and after a violent argument Tomás selected three of them and set off at once.

At the entrance to the level, the four men kneeled and made the sign of the cross. Then, holding their lamps high, they entered in single file. Soon their heads throbbed and their ears were buzzing. A hundred yards up ahead, the leader felt a thud on his back: the man behind him had fallen. They picked him up at once and carried him to safety, then found a replacement and again entered the passage.

About a hundred yards from the new workings, they found the first body. It was blown to pieces. A little further on, they tripped over a second, then a third, a fourth and a fifth. The last was that of the overseer, whom they recognized by his nail-studded boots. The inspector was missing. They hurried on.

Suddenly an enormous block fell thundering right in front of them, raising a great cloud of dust. It had to be cleared away. Soon after, they reached the spot of the explosion. For the most part, the wooden head-frames had been torn from the ceiling and twisted into a thousand crazy shapes. The men listened cautiously for sounds of an avalanche, but hearing none, they proceeded onward. Suddenly there was a sound of cracking and Tomás, at the head of the line, was struck on the shoulder. He nearly keeled over. He writhed in unbearable pain and was blinded by the dust, but managed to keep on. Now his teeth were chattering. He leapt upon a heap of stones over a yard high that blocked off the tunnel and began to remove the rubbish from that horrible tomb at a furious pace. His companions joined him, but after a great deal of work they found only three bodies.

Some of the rescuers gathered up the corpses while the others searched in the corners for the inspector. Perhaps the Devil had spirited him away.

"Here he is!" someone shouted.

They all ran over with their lamps. At one end of the tunnel, far back, a great bulk hung from the ceiling. It gave off the peculiar stench of burnt flesh. It was the body of the inspector. The point of a tremendous iron rod had pierced right through his stomach and stuck out more than a yard from his shoulders. The impact of the explosion had bent the rod and made it almost impossible to remove the body. Finally they managed to get it down.

Since the clothes he wore turned to ashes at the slightest touch, the men took off their shirts and respectfully covered him with them. In their simple souls there was not a vestige of hate or rancor. Marching forward, with the stretcher on their shoulders, they panted under the crushing weight of the dead man whose oppressive force still bore down upon them like a burdensome mountain on which Humanity and Time had piled pride, egoism and ferocity.

PAY DAY

Pedro María lay on his right side, legs folded under him, undercutting with blows of his pick the bottom of a vein. That cut, which miners call a rift, was now a foot deep, but the water which soaked down from the roof and over the face of the coal block filled the rift every five minutes. Then he would have to stop, set down his pickaxe and use his leather cap to scoop out the filthy liquid that now oozed under his body and later collected in puddles at the end of the gallery.

He had been at it for several hours, doing his utmost to complete the cutting. In that narrow rat hole, stripped to the waist in the almost unbearable heat, his sweating body gave off a warm sort of vapor that, mingled with the lampsmoke, formed about him a kind of thick mist that impeded his vision and made his task even more arduous and endless. The poor ventilation hampered him even more. The heavy, dust-laden air made him cough and choke in turn, while a bare three feet of working space allowed him to assume only those strained, uncomfortable positions that sent his limbs to sleep and brought on intolerable cramps and pains.

On his elbow, neck twisted, he hacked away doggedly, and at each blow the water hit at his face with great drops that struck his eyes like hammers. He stopped only to bail out. Then, oblivious of his aching muscles, the fetid air around him, and the mud into which his body had sunk, he seized his pickaxe and began again. Today, he knew, was the last of the fortnight, and he was obstinately resolved to remove as many carloads as possible. This idea was now so dominant in his thoughts and absorbed so much of his energy that the physical torture affected him like a spur digging into the flanks of a wild horse.

When the rift was finished, Pedro María, without a moment's rest, prepared to remove the coal. He tried out various positions, seeking the best one in which to attack the vein, but finally had to resign himself to working in the same way as before, on his right side, because this was the only way he could manage the pick-axe with relative ease. Removing the coal looks deceptively simple, but really requires great skill and dexterity. If the blow is hit at too sharp an angle, the pick slips and only small chunks are loosened. If the angle is not sharp enough, the steel point bounces off and gets as dull as a hoe.

Pedro María worked resolutely on the anthracite deposit over the rift. Each downward swing brought more shiny black chunks to the rapidly-mounting pile at his feet. But as he struck higher, he became more and more exhausted. There was not room enough to bear down on the pick. Pinned between wall and ceiling, it bit into the coal feebly and, despite his redoubled efforts, dislodged only a few small pieces of coal.

His body was drenched with sweat and a thick cloud of dust from the vein mingled with the air he breathed. It found its way into his throat and lungs and sent him into spasms of coughing that tore at his chest and left him breathless. But he kept on digging without letup, as if to fight the obstacle tooth and nail. And so furious had he become that, even at the risk of being walled up in there forever, he tore from the ceiling a large sustaining timber that kept getting in the way of his pick.

A swift, persistent drop of water began to trickle down his neck. At first it felt delightfully cool, but the pleasant sensation soon gave way to a burning itch. He squirmed sideways, but in vain, Before, it had trickled along the beam and disappeared down the wall, but now the insidious drop seared into his flesh like molten lead.

Nonetheless, he continued as before, unstinting in his efforts. As the coal piled up between his legs, he sought another good place in the block where he might dig. He had made so many holes, for so many years, in this wall which was always the same, and so thick it appeared endless.

Pedro María left work at nightfall. Taking his lamp, he dragged himself through the corridors, and finally reached the central haulageway. Air currents chilled his body as he stumbled along painfully on legs unsteady from so many hours of forced immobility.

A wild wind lashed his face when he reached the the platform outside. Undeterred, he hurried down the road without stopping.

Above his head great dark masses of clouds scurried before a strong north wind. The silvery moon, traveling in the opposite direction, shot into them with the violence of a projectile, turned pale, was lost; then, through a rent in their dense masses, it reappeared rapid and brilliant again. Then the darkness momentarily receded and on the ground the puddles of filthy roofwater reflected gleaming outlines. It his haste to get home to the healing warmth of his fireside, Pedro María did not bother to avoid them.

He entered the narrow room chilled to the bone, with his clothes sticking to his skin. A few coals were burning in the hearth, before which stretched a clothesline with a pair of pants and a shirt. These he put on without delay, after throwing the wet clothes he was wearing in the corner. Then his wife complained because today again she had been able to get nothing at the store. Pedro María did not answer. Nevertheless, his wife kept talking and explained to him that tonight he would have to go to bed without supper because they needed the little coffee they had for the following day. He interrupted her and said:

"No matter, woman. Tomorrow's pay day and our troubles will be over."

And now, dead tired, he stretched out on his miserable bed near the wall. It was made of four planks and two stools and covered over with old sacking. One dirty, threadbare blanket provided the only covering. His wife and two small children, one five and the other an eight-month-old baby, slept in a similar bed but more comfortably, since a straw mattress had been added to the sacking.

When the Company had cut off their provisions five days ago, they had been forced to sell or pawn the few clothes and kitchen utensils they had. In a place like this, off the beaten track, there was no place to buy excepting at the Company Store, where everyone had to make purchases by means of Company scrip or tokens.

Pedro María soon sank into a deep sleep. Within the four walls there was silence, interrupted only by occasional gusts of wind and rain outside that rattled the windows and door of the miserable room.

Pedro María awoke late in the morning. It was toward the end of June and a fine, persistent drizzle was falling from the leaden sky. A thick curtain of fog from the sea rolled in and shut off the horizon, like an opaque wall advancing slowly and devouring everything visible in its path.

Under the tin roofs of the porches, the women and children ran back and forth, and the barechested workers scrubbed their skin vigorously in order to rub off the coalsmut of a week's work. Pay day was always awaited anxiously and all faces were bright with anticipation.

When Pedro María had finished his weekly toilette, he stood for a while by the doorway, contemplating the downpour in silence. He was barely thirty-five, but his withered face, his sunken eyes and gray-streaked hair and beard made him look older than fifty.

For him had already begun the sad, fearful period when miners start to lose their strength, and with it, the courage and energy of ephemeral youth.

After having contemplated the gloomy landscape stretching out before him, he re-entered the room and sat down beside the fireplace. Water for coffee was boiling in the iron pot, and his wife who had gone out returned with some bread and sugar for breakfast. Although younger than her husband, she was already faded and worn by a life of work and privations which a nursing baby only made more difficult and painful.

When their scant meal was over, they both began to calculate how much he would receive in his pay envelope. What with correcting each other's estimates over and over again, they finally decided that, after taking care of their bill at the store, they would have enough left to redeem their kitchen utensils. This prospect made them happy. Since at this very moment the bell in the pay office began to ring, Pedro María put on his sandals and went out. He was followed by his wife who carried the baby in her arms and held the five-year-old by the hand as she walked along sinking her bare feet into the mud. They headed for the road where they joined the numerous groups that were all hastening toward the mine.

The wind and heavy downpour forced them to quicken their steps so that they might seek refuge under the roofs at the mine entrance, but soon the space was filled to capacity by the ever-increasing motley crowd.

All the personnel responsible for the various jobs around the mine was here, from the old foreman right down to the eight-year-old gate boy. They huddled together to avoid the water that was pouring down from the eaves, and stared intently at the closed window of the payteller.

After waiting a while, they saw the window raised. They began the pay-off. This operation was carried out in sections. The workers were called one by one by the foremen in charge of paywindows. As a rule the pay envelopes were almost empty, since they contained only the balance which remained after deductions of all kinds for fines and oil, coal and supplies bought from the Company Store.

The workers approached and withdrew in silence. Comments were forbidden; no reclamations could be made until after the last worker was paid. Sometimes a miner paled and gazed with fear and surpise at the money placed on the counter for him, not daring to touch it. But the foreman's cry of "Get back!" made him stretch out his hand and clutch the coins with trembling fingers, and then stand aside with his head lowered and a stupid, crestfallen expression on his face. His wife would come out to meet him anxiously, asking:

"How much did they give you?"

And the workman instead of answering would open his hand and show her the coins. Then they would look at each other silently, overwhelmed, feeling the earth rock beneath their feet.

All of a sudden, peals of laughter broke the silence. A miner, who had been handed a twenty-centavo piece by the cashier, took it, looked at it attentively for an instant as though it were some rare and curious object, and then flung it away in a rage. A swarm of ragamuffins pounced greedily on the coin, while the worker, hands in pockets, trudged down the road. An old woman ran behind him, with her skirts raised, shrieking "Juan, Juan!" at the top of her voice. But he did not stop and soon, lashed by wind and rain, they disappeared in the distance.

Pedro María awaited his turn patiently, and when the foreman shouted, "Pickmen from Doble," he shook nervously expecting to be called; but the three words of his name were not sounded. One after another his companions were called, and when once again he heard the foreman shout "Pickmen from Media Hoja," a shiver coursed through his body and his eyes dilated. His wife, surprised and fearful, turned and said:

"They haven't called you! Is something wrong?" And

since he would not answer, she began to wail and rocked the baby in her arms who, hungry and uncomfortable, had begun to cry desperately.

A neighbor approached and asked:

"Haven't they called him yet?"

And since the reply was in the negative, she added:

"They haven't called him either," and pointed to her son, a twelve-year-old boy so pale and skinny that he looked no more than eight.

She was a tall, good-looking young widow with a handsome face, red lips, and glistening white teeth. Now she leaned against the wall and looked daggers at the paywindow, behind which shone the blonde moustache and fleshy cheeks of the paymaster.

Meanwhile Pedro María tortured himself making calculation after calculation. But like so many others in the same predicament, he had not reckoned with unforeseen fines, cuts in salary, or the sudden and capricious rises in prices at the Company Store.

When the last worker from the last shift had reached the window, the gruff voice of the overseer resounded clear and vibrant:

"Complaints!"

And about a hundred men and women pushed forward, all of them impelled onward by the hope that their names had not appeared on the list because of some oversight or error.

At the head of the line stood the widow, holding her child by the hand. Her face neared the window.

"José Ramos, gate boy," she said.

"Hasn't he been called?"

"No, sir."

The cashier thumbed through the pages of the ledger and read curtly, "José Ramos, twenty-six days at twenty-five centavos. Has one peso in fines. Still owes fifty centavos at the Company Store."

"A peso in fines! What for? And it's not twenty-five centavos he earns but thirty-five."

The cashier did not take the trouble to answer her, but in an imperiously compelling voice shouted through the window: "Next!"

The young woman wanted to insist, but the overseers tore her away and shoved her violently outside the circle.

Her energetic nature came to the fore and her fury choked her as her eyes blazed.

"Thieving scum!" she shrieked hoarsely. And with her head thrown back and her body visible under her damp clothes, she remained momentarily poised and challenging, her dark eyes flashing with intense anger.

"Don't get angry, woman. It's a disgrace to God," proffered someone jokingly in the hubbub.

The woman veered like a lioness. "God!" she said. "For the poor there is no God." And casting a furious glance toward the paywindow, she exclaimed:

"A curse on you men without a conscience! May the earth swallow you up!"

The overseers smiled, and their eyes shone hungrily as they stared at the good-looking woman. The widow darted a defiant look at them all, and turned around toward her child, who gazed openmouthed at a flock of passing gulls.

"Get along, you fool," she shouted and gave him a hard shove.

The push was so hard and the little boy's legs so weak, that he fell face down in the mud. Seeing her child on the ground made the mother burst into tears. She bent hastily over and helped her son to his feet, kissing him lovingly and drying with her lips the tears that ran down his anemic cheeks.

Now it was Pedro María's turn. He was waiting restlessly by the paywindow. While the cashier turned the pages, Pedro María's heart thumped fast and furiously; the anguish of uncertainty gripped his throat like a hangman's noose. When the paymaster turned around and said to him, "You have ten pesos in fines and they've discounted twelve carloads which had slack in them; in addition, you owe three pesos to the Store," he wanted to answer but could not and just walked away with his arms limp at his sides, like a drunkard. His wife had only to glance at him to guess that he was empty-handed. She began to cry, stammering, while she hugged the baby in her arms convulsively:

"Holy Virgin, what are we going to do?"

And when her husband, anticipating her questions, said, "We owe three pesos to the Company Store," the unhappy woman wept twice as hard, and the two youngsters joined her. Silent and gloomy, Pedro María witnessed her despair. And at that moment, life seemed so vile to him, that if he could have found an easy way to free himself of it, he would have taken it without hesitation.

Misfortune seemed to issue from the paywindow. All those who approached, went away with drawn, convulsed faces, clenching their fists, muttering curses and oaths. And the rain kept on falling in an incessant downpour, drenching the earth and penetrating the clothes of those poor people for whom the downpour and the inclemencies of heaven were but a very small part of their work and suffering.

Pedro María, silent and frowning, saw his wife and children draw away, their rags clinging to their skinny bodies, making them look even more wretched. His first impulse had been to follow them, but a swift vision of the naked walls of the room, the cold hearth and the child asking for bread, kept him nailed to the spot. A few friends called out to him, with knowing looks, but he did not feel like drinking; his head was as heavy as lead on his shoulders and in his empty brain there was not a single thought or idea. An immense lassitude had benumbed his limbs. When he had found a dry place, he stretched out on the ground.

Much later, when he awoke, the streets were deserted and the raindrops still played their happy music, swiftly flowing down the roof gables.

THE DEVIL'S PIT

In a low narrow room, the overseer on duty, seated at his desk, before him a great open register, vigilantly kept count of the descending miners on that cold winter morning. Through the doorway could be seen the elevator awaiting its human load. Once filled, it disappeared noiselessly and rapidly down the damp hole of the shaft.

The miners arrived in small groups. While they took down the lighted lamps from hooks on the wall, the overseer fixed on each a penetrating glance, then with his pencil placed a dash by the name in his book. Suddenly, addressing two workers who were hurrying toward the exit, he stopped them with a gesture, saying:

"You wait."

Surprised, they turned with a vague, worried look on their pale faces. The younger of the two was a freckled lad of about twenty whose thick shock of reddish hair had earned him the nickname Copperhead. He was short, stocky and very muscular. The older, taller man was thin and bony with a weak, sickly appearance.

They held their lamps in one hand and in the other carried little pieces of string with glass beads or buttons of various forms and colors tied to the ends. These were the tallies which the miners fastened to each carload to indicate to those above the load count for each worker.

The clock on the wall slowly struck six. From time to time, a late miner would rush through the door all out of breath, grab his lamp, and casting a timid glance at the overseer, leave as hastily as he came in. The impassive, severe overseer, without uttering a word, would place a cross by the straggler's name.

After some moments of silent waiting, the overseer spoke:

"Aren't you workers from the Alta Mine?" he asked.

"Yes, sir, that we are," they answered.

"Sorry, but I'll have to fire you. I got orders to cut down on the number of workers in this cutting."

Neither of them answered. Finally, the old man said:

"But will we get something to do in another place?"

The overseer slammed his book shut, leaned back in his chair and replied gravely, "That'll be hard. We've got too many on all the jobs already."

"We'll take any job. We'll do timbering, planking, anything you want," he insisted.

The overseer shook his head. "I've already told you there are too many, and if we don't get some more orders to ship, we'll have to lay off miners in the other cuttings, too."

The miner's lips tightened in a wry smile. "Why not be honest, Don Pedro," he exclaimed. "You might as well come out with it. You just want to force us to work in the Devil's Pit."

The overseer jumped up, protesting indignantly:

"No one forces anyone here. You're perfectly free to turn down any job that doesn't suit you. And the Company has just as much right to do whatever it thinks profitable."

They listened without answering, and the overseer, noting the subdued expression on their faces, softened his tone.

"Although I've been given final orders," he added, "I'd like to help you out. There are two openings for diggers in the new level or the Devil's Pit, as you call it. You could fill them right away. Tomorrow may be too late."

Copperhead and his friend exchanged a knowing

glance. These were old tactics and they knew all the time
what was coming. But they seemed resigned to their fate.
There was no way to avoid it. Between starving and
being crushed by a cave-in, the latter was definitely
preferable. It had the advantage of being quick. And
besides, where could they go? Winter, the implacable
enemy of poor people, which converted little streams into
raging torrents, had left the fields desolate and barren.
The lowlands were immense swamps of muddy water
and on the hills and mountain sides the trees beneath
an eternally murky sky displayed the barrenness of their
bare branches and trunks.

In the farmers' huts, starvation loomed. It could be
seen on the ravenous faces of the inhabitants who found
themselves obliged to knock on the doors of workshops
and factories searching for the daily bread which the
sterile, musty soil of their unproductive fields denied
them.

So they had to submit, to fill the vacancies that this
Devil's Pit constantly opened in the files of weak unfor-
tunates who spent their lives in constant struggle against
the adversities of fortune, abandoned by all and against
whom any injustice and indignity was permitted.

The matter was settled. Without objection the two
men accepted the new job. A moment later, they were
in the cage, hurtling into the depths of the mine.

The workings known as the Devil's Pit had a sinister
reputation. They had been opened up in order to extract
the mineral from a newly discovered vein, and although
the work had begun with all due precaution, as the miners
penetrated further into the rock, it had become increasingly
porous. The seepage, rare at first, was now steadily
increasing, endangering the ceiling which was maintained
only by constant reinforcement. But re-timbering was
costly and sent the price of coal sky-high. The Company
did less and less of this most essential work with only a
minimum of timbers, economizing all they could.

The results of this system were soon felt. Miners

were often carried out bruised, wounded or crushed by cave-ins. The ceiling, dangerously weakened by water, was a constant threat to life. Terrified, the miners began to refuse assignments in the deadly tunnel. The Company soon persuaded them to continue work by adding a few extra pennies to their pay envelopes. Thus the exploitation of the new vein continued.

A short while later, however, the wage increase was cancelled; it was possible to get the same results by recruiting workers the way the overseer had that morning.

Copperhead reached home that night later than usual. Serious, thoughtful, he answered his mother's loving questions about the day's work with a curt monosyllable. In that humble abode there reigned a certain decency and cleanliness not known in most of those squalid hovels where, in repulsive propinquity, men, women, children and animals lived crowded together so that each one of the rooms brought to mind the biblical vision of Noah's Ark.

The miner's mother was a tall, thin, white-haired woman. She had a sweet resigned expression on her pale face which softened the light in her moist eyes always just on the brink of tears. She was called María de los Angeles.

The daughter and mother of miners, terrible misfortunes had aged her prematurely. Her husband, her two sons, one after the other, killed by the cave-ins and the firedamp explosions, were the tribute that she and hers had paid to the insatiable greed of the mine. All she had left was that one boy for whom her still-young heart beat in constant dread. Always fearful of some accident, her imagination never left for a moment the dark shadows of that layer of coal that absorbed the existence of her only happiness, the only tie which held her to life.

How often in thoughtful moments she had wondered, without ever reaching a solution, about the odious human inequalities which condemned the poor, the majority, to sweat blood in order to sustain the luxury and pomp of the useless existence of the few. If only she might live without the perpetual anxiety over her loved ones, whose lives were the price, paid over and over again, of their daily bread.

But those meditations were transitory and, not being able to decipher the enigma, the old woman avoided such thoughts and returned to her chores with her usual melancholia.

While she finished preparing supper, she noticed that Copperhead was still sitting quietly by the fireplace. His silence made her feel uneasy, and she was just about to question him when she heard the door open and saw a young woman's face in the doorway.

"Good evening, dear," she said. "How is he getting along?"

"The same," replied the young woman entering the room. "The doctor says the bone in his leg hasn't knitted yet and that he has to stay in bed without moving."

The newcomer was thin, with a dark, gaunt-looking face. In her right hand she held a tin bowl and struggled to avoid looking at the steaming soup on the table.

María de los Angeles continued questioning as she took the bowl and filled it. "And have you spoken to the bosses? Have they given you any aid?"

"Yes, I was there. They told me I had nothing coming to me, that they did enough in giving us the room; but that if he died, I should go to the store and make out an order for four candles and a shroud." And with a sigh she added, "I pray my poor Juan won't make them go to that expense."

María de los Angeles handed her the soup and a piece of bread besides. "The Virgin will repay you," called the woman as she walked toward the door.

"Poor Juana," said the mother. "It's almost a month now since they brought him up from the mine with a broken leg. What was his job?"

"He was a digger in the Devil's Pit," answered her son who had drawn his chair to the table.

"Ah, yes. They say that miners who work there take their lives into their own hands."

"It's not that bad, Mother. It's different now that so many major repair jobs have been done. Nothing's gone wrong for over a week."

"Maybe that's so, but I couldn't go on living if you worked there. I'd prefer to go begging through the fields. I don't want them to bring you home one day the way they brought your father and your brothers." Huge teardrops slid down her withered cheeks.

Copperhead said no more and ate without lifting his eyes from his plate.

When he went to work the following morning, he had still not told her about the new job. There would always be plenty of time to pass on the bad news to her. Like most boys his age, he did not place much importance in his mother's fears, and believed it useless to struggle against what destiny held in store.

When, an hour after her son's departure, Maria opened the door, she was enchanted by the radiant clarity that flooded the fields. She had not seen such a beautiful morning for a long time. A golden halo circled the sun as it rose above the horizon flooding the wet land with bright rays. On all sides rose white and blue vapor. The sun's light, soft as a caress, gave a breath of life to dead nature. There in the distance, flocks of birds crossed the serene blue sky and on his little mound of sand, a cock, his iridescent feathers gleaming in the light, cried out a strident alarm each time the shadow of a bird went by him.

Several old men, leaning on canes or crutches, appeared on the dirty porches, attracted by the glorious splendor that lit up the whole landscape. They walked slowly, stretching their cramped limbs, eager for that soft warmth that radiated from on high. They were the mine's invalids, the defeated ones. There were but few

left now who had not lost either a leg or an arm. They
sat on a long wooden bench where the full rays of the
sun hit them. Their tired eyes, all sunken in their sockets,
held a strange, fixed expression. Not a word passed
between them, but from time to time, after a dry, racking
cough, their closed lips opened and they spat up a phlegm
that was black as ink.

It was almost noon. In their tenements the women
were busy preparing the lunch baskets for their men when
a short blast on the alarm siren sent them all scurrying
out of their homes in terror.

The siren had stopped and there was no outward
indication of catastrophe. Everything looked as usual
and from the great chimney still escaped the great plume
of smoke that stretched out impelled by the breeze toward
the sea.

María de los Angeles was just about to put the bottle
of coffee into her son's lunch basket when the alarm siren
blew. Dropping everything, she ran to the door past
which the women, skirts raised high, were frantically
rushing, followed by crowds of children running desperately after their mothers. The old woman followed their
example. Her feet seemed to sprout wings; the spur of
terror galvanized her old muscles and her whole body
vibrated and quivered like the string of a full-drawn bow.

Soon she was leading the throng and her white hair,
glistening in the sun, seemed to draw after it the sombre
mass of the ragged flock. The tenements were deserted.
Doors and windows banged open and shut in the wind.
A dog, tied on one of the porches, sat back on his
haunches, head high, and howled mournfully as if in
answer to the distant clamor.

Only the old men, on their sun-drenched bench,
remained silent and motionless, in the same attitude, eyes
fixed on an invisible beyond, immune to anything that
went on about them save that radiant warmth that filtered
into their tired bodies a little of the energy and heat
that quickens life in the barren fields.

As little chicks, suddenly aware of a descending hawk, run peeping for shelter under the hen's raised wings, so these groups of women, hair streaming, wailing, overcome by terror, soon appeared under the upraised arms of the hoist, pushing and straining on the wet platform. Mothers hugged close their tiny children wrapped in dirty rags against their half-bare breasts. An inhuman clamor rose from their half-opened mouths all twisted in grief.

At the same time, part of the crowd went crashing into the wooden fence that protected one side of the shaft opening, and on the other side, several taciturn, gloomy-faced miners held them back. There were deafening shouts for news of relatives, the number of men dead, and the place where the catastrophe had occurred.

Then one of the engineers appeared in the doorway of the engine room. He was a fat Englishman with red sidewhiskers and a pipe clenched in his teeth. He regarded the mob with customary indifference. Hundreds of voices turned their fury on him:

"Murderers! Murderers!" they shouted.

The women lifted their arms over their heads and brandished their clenched fists in the air, and the Englishman, whose appearance had provoked this explosion of hatred, blew several puffs of smoke on his pipe and then turned his back and disappeared.

The news circulated by the workers quieted the excitement somewhat: there were only three dead, as yet unidentified, and as for the rest, there was hardly any need to ask. There had been a cave-in in the Devil's Pit where men had been working for two hours to remove the victims and they expected, at any moment now, the signal to hoist.

This report brought new hope into many an anxious heart. María de los Angeles leaned against the barricade; she felt the hook that had been clawing her insides loosen its iron grip. Hers was not hope, but certainty: surely her son was one of the dead. And with the fierce egoism of a mother, she listened almost indifferently to the hysterical sobbing of the women.

Meanwhile the hours flew by and beneath the clay and brick arches the motionless machine relaxed its iron members in the darkness of the vast tunnels. The cables, like the tentacles of an octopus, rose quivering from the deep shaft and curled round the winding drums their flexible, slimy arms.

The packed, compact, human mass palpitated and moaned like a bleeding, dying beast but up above, over the vast plain, the afternoon sun cast its brilliant warm rays. A heavenly calm and serenity reigned in the concave mirror of the diaphanous, blue sky, unmarred by a single cloud.

Suddenly, the women stopped crying. The bell rang once, followed by three peals that resounded slowly. The crowd stared eagerly at the ascending cable, and waited. At the end of it lay that terrible unknown which they awaited so anxiously, yet feared to discover.

An occasional sob broke the silence on the platform, and the faraway howl that spread over the plain pierced every heart like a death omen.

There was quite a lapse of time before the huge iron ring that crowned the cage appeared above the edge of the shaft. The elevator wavered momentarily, then stopped. It had been secured by hooks at the top.

Inside, several bareheaded miners stood about a small cart black with clay and coaldust.

A tremendous clamor greeted the appearance of the death cart. The mob closed in, greatly hindering the removal of the bodies. The first one lay wrapped in blankets with only its two stiff, mud-caked, bare feet protruding. The second was a bareheaded old man with white hair and a beard.

The third and last came into view. Through the folds of the cloth around him protruded several strands of red hair that glittered in the sunlight like newly smelted copper. Several voices whispered in awe, "Copperhead!"

They lifted the body by the shoulders and feet and placed it on the waiting stretcher.

When María de los Angeles saw that livid face and bloodsoaked hair, she made a superhuman effort to throw herself on him. But, hemmed in between the crowd and the fence, all she could do was reach out her arms and utter a piercing, inarticulate scream.

Then she felt all her strength give way. Her arms fell limply at her sides, and she stood rooted to the ground as if struck by a thunderbolt.

The crowd began to disperse, and as they left, several turned their faces toward the woman who, with her head sunken on her chest, completely unaware of anything about her, seemed absorbed in the contemplation of the open abyss at her feet.

* * *

No one ever found out how she had managed to jump the fence. Stopped by the cross cables, she was seen for one instant kicking her thin old legs in the empty air and then, without a cry, she disappeared into the abyss. Seconds later a muted sound, distant and scarcely audible, issued forth from the hungry mouth of the shaft from which escaped puffs of tenuous vapor: it was the breath of the monster gorged with blood in the depths of his den.

THE WELL

With her sleeves rolled high and a bucket of water perched on her head, Rosa crossed the space between the house and the garden. The fence of old boughs and dried-up tree trunks stood out dark, almost black, against the sandy soil of the dusty yard.

Rosa's face was all aglow with the freshness of youth and the soft warmth of ripe, unpicked fruit. Long eyelashes shaded her roguish green eyes, and when she smiled, the sensuous curve of her lips revealed her gleaming white teeth. Her arms, raised aloft to balance the bucket, accentuated her firm inciting breasts, and her blue percale skirt swung suggestively to the rhythm of her strong, shapely hips.

She entered the small vegetable garden by the little gate. With her back to the entrance, she began spraying the withered vegetables with handfuls of water which she scooped up from the bucket. So engrossed had she become that she failed to notice the young man who had just tiptoed through the half-opened gate and was advancing slyly towards her.

Dark fiery eyes lit up the pale, beardless face of this very young newcomer. The light down on his upper lip and the straight black hair that fell down over his narrow forehead gave him a childish look. He wore a blue and white striped shirt, grey pants and hemp sandals.

The slight rustling of leaves along the ground made

the girl turn rapidly. Surprise and obvious disdain appeared on her expressive face.

The visitor stopped before the beds of cabbages and lettuce that separated him from the girl and stood still, devouring her with his eyes.

She wiped her hands on the folds of her skirt with lowered eyes and a frown on her forehead.

"Rosa," said the young man with a laughing, jovial tone that scarcely hid his ill-controlled emotion, "you turned just in time. What a surprise I was going to give you!"

Then, changing his tone, with an insinuating passionate voice, he went on:

"Now that we are alone, tell me, what have they said about me? Why won't you listen to me? Why do you hide when I want to see you?"

Rosa kept quiet but her annoyance obviously increased. His amorous complaints now became tender and he pleaded:

"Why should you scorn the love of a heart that is yours? Remember, we were sweethearts and you loved me."

Still without raising her eyes, Rosa replied:

"I never told you so!"

"That's right, but you never shied away when I talked of love. And on the day I asked you to marry me you didn't say no. On the contrary, you laughed and said yes with your eyes."

"I thought it was a joke."

A forced smile hovered over his lips and in reproachful tones he exclaimed:

"A joke! Even though they laugh at me for being in such a hurry, I gave my word and I'm going to get the priest right now to marry us."

Rosa's impatience and annoyance had increased to such a point that her only reply was to pick up her bucket and head for the gate. But the young man stopped her.

"You won't leave until you've told me why you've changed."

The blood rose to his pale face, his eyes glistened and his voice trembled with disappointment and anger.

"Ah! you bitch! I know who's changed you. But before he gets what he wants, by God, I'll tear out his tongue and soul!"

Sullen and unrelenting, Rosa stood straight and still.

"For the last time. Do you or do you not want to be my wife?"

"Never!" was her fierce reply. "I'll die first!"

The scornful look which accompanied these words and the open defiance in the green, shining eyes stunned him for a minute. But, suddenly, drunk with despair and desire, he jumped at the girl, grabbed her by the waist, raised her high in the air and then threw her on the ground. A violent struggle ensued. Rosa, who was strong and vigorous, resisted desperately, clawing and biting the hand that tried to cut off her screams for help.

An unexpected arrival saved her. A second young man stood in the gateway. The attacker leaped up and with clenched fists awaited the intruder, who bore down on him with a menacing look and bloodshot eyes.

Rosa, cheeks aflame and wet with angry tears, stood to one side by the fence. Ashamed and sobbing, she covered modestly with her neckerchief the hidden beauties revealed by her torn waist.

Meanwhile, the two youths were fighting to the death. The very first blows showed the strength and ability of the two combatants. The girl's defender was a stalwart youth. He was a head taller than his antagonist, with broad shoulders and a deep chest, curly hair, light eyes and a blond moustache. Remigio, the more delicate of the two, fought with astounding agility, sidestepping the savage blows that his enemy rained upon him and returning blow for blow, strong and erect on his sturdy legs. He emitted a panting whistle of rage each time his adversary's fist hit his swollen, perspiring face.

Rosa, pulling the dry leaves from her jet-black, wavy hair, watched the progress of the fight with flaming eyes. It went on with unabated fury, neither side gaining an advantage. The champions redoubled their attacks before the girl, like wild beasts fighting over the possession of an exciting female.

The vegetable beds were trampled beyond repair and the girl looked aghast at the destruction. Her anger increased and in the instant that her aggressor passed in front of her, pursued by his formidable adversary, she had an inspiration. Stooping over, she caught up a handful of dirt and threw it into his face. The effect was instantaneous. He vacillated and in one second was knocked down, where he lay with the victor's knee upon his chest.

Rosa cast one last glance in their direction, and then she ran quickly to the house, not even stopping for her empty bucket. There she turned once more and distinguished the vanishing figures —her protector headed off one way while the defeated suitor disappeared in the opposite direction— hastily putting distance between themselves and their battleground.

The young girl slid along the almost deserted tenement porches past a whole series of doors until she reached a half-open one. Softly pushing it, she crossed the threshold. A great fire burned in the fireplace and in the center of the room squatted a woman washing clothes in a wooden tub.

Miserable poverty was written all over the bare whitewashed walls. A tainted odor arose from the bits of trash that were thrown around the floor and into the corners. A table and a few chairs comprised the only furniture. Behind the door could be seen the railing of a stairway that led to a second room upstairs.

Without interrupting her work, the middle-aged woman, who was big and had a pockmarked, blotchy face, fixed a penetrating eye on the girl and exclaimed with some surprise:

"What's the matter. What's happened to you?"

Rosa answered with a tearful, repentant voice:

"Oh, mama, the garden is ruined. The cabbages, the lettuce and the radishes have all been pulled up and trampled on."

The woman's face turned purple.

"Damn you," she shrieked, "you must have left the gate open and that neighbor's pig must have gotten in."

She stood up brandishing her plump arms and let go a whole string of curses and threats.

"If it's true, I'll tan your hide!"

And swishing up her skirts, she ran quickly to verify the disaster.

The air was hot and heavy and the sun at its zenith in the leaden, misty sky. Sunken footsteps left whitish trails in the gray, shifting sand.

Rosa, following her mother, looked all about with anxious, searching eyes and after a moment discovered, above a bush, the head of someone who was hiding. She smiled. She saw that the hidden onlooker was her defender. He leaned out a little and blew her a kiss. The young girl blushed and her eyes shone. In spite of the fact that she knew, given her mother's violent temper, that a good beating awaited her, she happily entered the ill-fated garden from which emanated a formidable chorus of wails, curses and imprecations.

An only child, Rosa helped her mother at home, while the father, and old miner, struggled pitifully underground to earn the miserable pay that provided their daily bread.

Although she was just a simple miner's daughter, Rosa was a real beauty, with a certain shy virtue that had rejected, up to now, all advances of the many suitors who would have given anything for that healthy body, exuberant with life, with its irresistible grace of a mature woman.

Of those who ardently courted her, there stood out two handsome youths of opposite type. Of all the Don

Juans in the mine, they were the cream of the crop. Both had set out to win the beautiful Rosa. She received their passionate declarations with giggles, mocking airs and funny roguish faces. These two young men had been friends since childhood, but this love had severed their friendship and ended up by separating them completely.

For a time, Remigio, who hauled coal in the mine, seemed to enjoy whatever small favors this disdainful young girl apportioned her ardent suitors. But that did not last long and the enamored youth saw with bitter deception that the coal digger, Valentín, his blond rival, was taking his place in the lovely Rosa's fickle heart. Although, at first, she had listened smilingly to his impassioned protests, encouraging him at times with an enticing look, of late she had begun to avoid him and on the few occasions when he did get a chance to talk to her, he could scarcely get an evasive, cool and disgusted word or two in' reply.

The girl's indifference only served to fire his passion. Eaten by jealousy, he redoubled his efforts to regain the lost territory, futilely attempting to overcome the growing indifference of the girl, who each day showed clearly her preference for the other. The rivalry of the two youths grew and the mutual hatred rankling in their breasts made them irreconcilable enemies. They watched each other vigilantly, never missed an opportunity to stop each other from getting an advantage.

This siege on their daughter's amorous attentions did not bother her parents in the least. Whether she gave in or not was a matter for her to decide.

Remigio, the rejected suitor, wanted an explanation from the young girl to end the uncertainty that tormented him. For that reason, he decided not to go to the mine one morning. Valentín, who learned of this, fearing his motive, resolved to spy upon his rival. The consequence had been the encounter in the garden and the terrible fight that followed.

Rosa, immature still, had at first received willingly

and coquettishly Remigio's amorous insinuations. She was flattered that the conquest had roused the envy of her friends. But soon, the vehemence of his love and his ardent gaze filled with passion and desire made her tremble. Her fear, stronger than her own awakening senses, gave her, when he was present, a feeling of repulsion.

But not so with Valentín. She blushed when she saw him. If he spoke to her, the ready, witty and cutting remarks, with which she could stop the most daring young man, never reached her lips. She would stammer a monosyllable or two and then bashfully scurry away.

The youth's open, frank face, his happy, ebullient nature drew her insensibly to him. The seed of love, that had until then been hidden deep in her being, found fertile soil in that virgin breast.

After the fight that day, the actions of the two rivals changed. Valentín now openly courted Rosa. Remigio watched from a distance. His passion, fed by jealousy and scorn, was a raging, consuming fire. He spent his time dreaming up the most terrible, monstrous and quick way to avenge her unfaithful, traitorous love.

Rosa, completely absorbed by her new love, paid little or no attention to him. If she felt anything at all, it was a rather scornful indifference.

So things went on for some time. The garden plot had been replanted, but it was never known who had destroyed it nor what had happened there. Then, one day, Rosa's father had a wonderful idea. As the water for spraying had to be carried from a great distance, he decided to dig a well next to the fence. His wife and daughter heartily encouraged him in his new project. It would not be too difficult because the land was of black thick sand that was quite deep. About twelve feet down one struck water which kept its level all year round. Work was to be begun on the next Sunday and all their friends offered to help. The most enthusiastic were Remigio and Valentín.

The designated day arrived and they began work early in the morning. The excavation was made near the gate and by noon they had dug six feet. A pulley on a wooden frame had been erected and the sand was hauled up in a big iron bucket tied to the end of the rope.

The two rivals worked the hardest but they kept out of each other's way. When one was at the bottom filling the bucket, the other stayed up top shoveling away the sand from the opening. Taking advantage of a moment when Remigio was down below, Valentín, pretending he was thirsty, threw down his shovel and headed for Rosa's house. She was at the door sewing.

"I've come to ask for a glass of water. I'm dying of thirst," he said in a light malicious tone.

Rosa rose silently, her eyes shining, went to the corner and came back with the glass. Valentín took both the glass and her small brown hand into his own.

Blushing and smiling, she cried, "Watch out! You'll spill it!"

Never taking his eyes off her, he swallowed the water in one gulp, wiped his mouth on his sleeve, then added:

"If every time I wanted to see you, Rosa, I had to drink a glass of water, I'd willingly drink the whole ocean."

She laughed showing her white teeth.

"Salt and all?"

"Yes, salt, fish, boats and all!"

"What big swallows!" and she laughed heartily at his joke.

Just then, a voice from upstairs called:

"Rosa, who's there?"

"It's Valentín, Mama."

They heard an indifferent "Oh!" and then all was silent.

Valentín had encircled her waist and now he drew her toward him. With her hands on his broad chest, Rosa pushed him away, murmuring softly and pleadingly:

"Go away! Leave me alone!"

Her breath came and went and her heart beat like a trip-hammer.

Ardently he whispered, "Rosa, my darling, my lovely dove!"

No longer able to resist, she looked passionately and longingly at him. Her arms gave way as she felt his hot breath. Throwing back her head, she closed her eyes. He hungrily kissed those fresh lips, redder than flowers, sweeter than honey.

A heavy step on the creaky staircase made them draw hastily apart. He left the room, shouting nonchalantly:

"Thanks, Rosa, see you later."

All atremble, Rosa tried to sew but she was so excited, she pricked her finger time and again.

On his way back to the well, Valentín, jubilant over his almost certain conquest, could not help throwing a triumphant glance at Remigio. One of the men shouted:

"How was the water? Did you quench your thirst?"

"God knows more than you and snoops less," was Valentín's sententious reply as he twirled his blond moustache.

By late afternoon, the well was finished. It was over twelve feet deep and six feet in diameter. The water was beginning to bubble slowly at the bottom. The workers left for the shady porch where they were to make the wooden frame that would keep the walls of the well from caving in. Remigio stayed behind to fix the pulley. He was about to join the others when the sight of Rosa's blue skirt through the bushes made him change his mind. Grabbing the rope, he slid quickly into the hole without being seen.

Rosa, who was on her way to pick some vegetables, paused by the well to see whether or not the water had begun to rise. Remigio waited quiet and still against the damp wall. Rosa came cautiously to the edge and peeked down. Surprised at first, she then smiled roguishly, grabbed the rope, pulled up the bucket and tied the rope firmly to the frame.

Remigio did not try to stop her. He had caught sight of her face as she leaned over. The little joke seemed a favorable sign to him. So he looked up and patiently waited for the end of the little game.

A minute or so later, Remigio heard a muffled exclamation and the sound of a struggle. Listening intently, he discerned a soft, harmonious voice murmuring hesitant, pleading words while a deep, masculine voice answered them passionately. The noise seemed to be moving away. He heard the gate bang shut. Then the crackling of leaves, and silence...

Remigio turned pale as a ghost. His muscles twitched and he gnashed his teeth. As he had recognized, Valentin's voice, he flew into an uncontrollable rage and began pounding the damp wall with his bare fists, crazed with anger and desperation.

Suddenly, he felt as though he had been pierced by a sharp dagger. Over his head heard a little soft scream—like the swish of a bird's wings. His blood boiled and his blurred eyes saw red. He suffered the tortures of hell while above him, through the hot and suffocating air, rose and fell the rhythmic symphony of fiery, interminable kisses. He clawed his breast until the blood ran. The little piece of blue sky above reminded him of the deep, clear eyes that were now reflecting another man's image.

Finally the hinges of the gate creaked. A rapid whispering followed by the sound of a last kiss wounded the ears of the prisoner below. An instant later he heard the steps of someone who stopped at the edge of the hole. A shadow appeared on the wall of the well and a jibing voice from above uttered an ironic and mortal insult.

A roar escaped from Remigio's breast; he turned deathly pale and his flaming eyes measured the distance between himself and his opponent who, laughing loudly, undid the rope and let it slide down over the pulley .

Remigio's first impulse was to rush up after his enemy

but a sudden fainting spell overtook him. When he had recovered a bit, he was about to ascend, when a slight vibration, caused by the galloping of a horse who was being chased by a dog near the opening, made pieces of the wall fall and the sand came up to his knees, completely covering the iron bucket.

The idea of being buried alive without being able to quench his thirst for rabid revenge gave him new strength. Agile as an acrobat, he climbed the rope to the top of the excavation. Free now, he hesitated as to which direction he would take. All about him extended the dry monotonous plain under the pale blue sky that the sun in its flight to the horizon was tinging with gold. The air was hot as fire and the sand burned like the hot ashes of an immense blast furnace. A hundred paces away rose the white rows of workers' houses surrounded by their little gardens protected by the brush fences.

What work and patience each one of those little enclosures represented! The topsoil carted from a great distance and spread in thin layers was a precious material whose preservation occasioned, at times, heated disputes and even bloody fights.

Remigio, seized now by an infinite sadness, gazed out over the landscape and he found it gloomy and sombre. The horse which had almost caused a cave-in was still galloping off there in the distance, raising great clouds of dust. But soon the memory of his injuries overcame his depression and his needling desire for revenge awoke in his untamed and semi-barbarous soul the implacable fury of his savage passions.

No punishment seemed too severe for those who had so cruelly laughed at his love and he swore never to miss a chance for revenge. Absorbed in these thoughts, he headed for the houses. Although his love had turned to hate, he still felt a strong desire to see Rosa, to find on her face, once so beloved, traces of the other's caresses.

He quickly crossed the space between the well and the houses. In front of Rosa's, her father and various

other men were nailing together the frame for the well.
Remigio stopped at a corner from which he could see
what went on. Before the door, her shapely arms bare
to the elbow, she was wringing clothes which she took
from a pail on the ground. Valentín leaned possessively
in the doorway. She met all his comments with a happy,
pleased response. Her fresh laughter pierced Remigio's
heart. Their happiness only increased the fury in his
breast. Rosa's face shone with joy and her shining eyes
held an expression of passionate languor that enhanced
her brilliant beauty.

When the last piece was wrung, Rosa picked up her
pail and headed for one of the yards followed by Valentín, who carried the clothesline which he fastened for her.
Then he helped her hang the clothes. Unaware that they
were being spied upon, they went on with their amorous
banter, free now from the curious eyes on the porches.
Suddenly, Valentín caught sight of his enemy, twenty
paces away. Wanting to make him feel the full weight of
his loss and the fullness of his own triumph, he put his
arm about the girl's neck, bent her head back and kissed
her full on the mouth. Then he whispered in her ear.

Remigio saw her turn quickly toward him; she
looked him up and down and then burst into boisterous
laughter. Freeing herself from her lover's arms, she ran
away doubled over with glee.

The offended youth stood there nailed to the spot.
He turned fiery red to the very roots of his hair. Blinded
by rage, he advanced a few steps, swaying like a drunkard.

On his way already to the well, Valentín was singing
at the top of his lungs:

"The fool who falls in love,
A dolt indeed is he;
He works and heats the water,
But another drinks the tea."

Remigio followed him with a wild look in his eye. A single thought obsessed him: KILL and then die too. In his crazed condition, he felt strong enough to overcome a giant.

Valentín had stopped at the edge of the well to pull up the bucket, but seeing that he could not free it from the mud that covered it, he slipped down to the bottom. When Remigio saw him disappear, he stopped a moment, at a loss, but then a sinister smile played about his lips and he hastened forward, undid the rope which ran over the pulley and down into the well. Now his enemy was a prisoner and in his power. But how to destroy him? He looked all about trying to find a weapon, a stone, anything; but just then, he caught sight of the horse's hoofprints. A memory, a distant idea came back to him. Oh, if he could only set a hundred horses pounding over that shifting soil! Strange visions of vengeance, torture and atrocious punishment swarmed through his over-excited brain. Suddenly a shiver ran over him. An inspiration, rapid as a lightning bolt, had crossed his mind. A hundred yards from there, behind one of the gardens, was a little square. About a hundred workmen were gathered there, playing games, darts, cards. He could hear distinctly their voices, shouts and loud laughter. There was what he needed and it took only a second to formulate his plan.

The day was ending and the shadows lengthening, when suddenly before the men appeared Remigio, his arms held high in a gesture of complete panic. In a thundering voice he shrieked:

"The well is caving in! The well is caving in!"

The men turned in surprise. Those who were lying down sprang to their feet. They all fixed astonished eyes on Remigio but no one moved. But when they heard him repeat:

"The well is caving in! Valentín is down there!" they understood and the human avalanche hurled itself toward the well.

Meanwhile, Valentín, completely unaware of the danger he was in, had dug up the bucket which Rosa's mother wanted back. The fallen rope which he knew he owed to his spiteful rival, whose footsteps he had heard, did not bother him. He knew that within a matter of moments they were coming to put in the well frame and would get him out. But when he heard the distant roar, and the sentence: "The well is caving in!" he felt the first brush of fear and the danger of an unknown menace made his heart take an extra beat.

The crowd bore down like a great landslide. Valentín saw with dismay that the walls were beginning to give way. The sand slid down like thick black liquid and piled up round his legs. He screamed. The whole earth shook suddenly, and around the top of the well a circle of heads peered anxiously down.

A hoarse howl escaped from Valentín's throat:

"For God's sake, fellows, get me out of here!"

The sand now reached his chest and, like water in a bucket, it began to rise slowly and silently all about him.

The crowd was growing thicker. The workmen pushed and jostled in an effort to see what was going on. Noise of their shouting filled the air. Everyone gave advice at the same time. Some called for ropes and others screamed:

"No, no —bring planks!"

A rope had been slung under Valentín's arms and they pulled furiously but the sand would not let go. It held on with invisible tentacles that encircled the victim's body in a damp and terrible embrace. Some older workmen tried in vain to disperse the avid crowd. The tramping on that shifting ground would only precipitate the catastrophe. The shout, "The well is caving in!" had emptied the houses. Men, women and children ran, collaborating, without knowing it, in Remigio's sinister plan. He, ferocious and gloomy, with his arms crossed, stood contemplating from a distance the success of his stratagem.

Rosa fought uselessly to get to the edge. Her penetrating, anguished cries rang out above the general clamor, but no one paid the slightest attention to her desperation and the human wall became with each instant more impassable.

Suddenly, there was a disturbance. A terrified, disheveled old woman split the crowd as they gave way to let her pass. Her wail filled the air:

"My son, my dear son!"

She reached the edge and, without a second's hesitation, she threw herself into the well. With indescribable terror Valentín cried:

"Mama, get me out of here!"

The implacable tide, slowly rising, never stopping, now reached his neck. Then, as though the weight above had suddenly increased, there was a new cave-in. That frightful head, its hair on end, suddenly disappeared and the hoarse cry of agony was instantly silenced. But, a moment later, it appeared again, eyes straining from their sockets, the open mouth full of mud. The mother, clawing like a person possessed, had succeeded in uncovering the livid face of her son. A horrible struggle went on about the blond head of the suffering youth. The old woman, howling with fear and madness, was on her knees holding back the inexorable tide with hands, arms and her whole body when the final cave-in took place.

The crust of earth above, undermined from below, was breaking up in various places. Those who were near the edge of the well felt the earth give way beneath their feet and they rolled in a confused mass into the hole. The well had collapsed completely. The old mother was buried to the shoulders more than three feet above Valentín's head.

When, after an hour of frantic and difficult digging, they brought out the body, the sun had already finished its course. Shadows filled the plain and from the west an immense sheaf of red, violent and orange rays rose from beneath the horizon and spread out fanwise toward the zenith.

JUAN FARIÑA

(Legend)

On the small promontory which is surrounded by the blue waters of the gulf, there may be seen today the ruined structures of the old colliery.

The tall brick chimneys rise above the dilapidated sheds which cover the rusty remains of the machines that now rest motionless on their rock foundations. The pistons no longer advance and retreat in their cylinders and the enormous flywheel, stopped in its career, seems like the wheel of a vehicle stuck forever on that pile of debris all eaten away by time

At the highest point, dominating the watery vastness, the tipple silhouettes the black lines of its crossbeams against the blue background of the sky like a sinister and mysterious cipher.

On the rough hillsides, the workers' houses show their sunken roofs and through the gaping windows and doors, all torn from their hinges, may be seen the white cracked walls of the deserted rooms.

Some years back, this solitary spot was the seat of a powerful colliery. Life and movement animated this mine where today nothing may be heard but the swish of the waves as they strike the foot of the mountain. Dense columns of smoke once rose from the enormous chimneys and the rhythmic beat of the machinery, together with the rising and descending of the elevators in the shaft, was never interrupted. Down here in the homes ranged on the sides of the hills, the voices of women and the merry shouts of children were caught up in the roar of the sea so that the place was always noisy and turbulent.

One January morning, while the machinery jetted forth its labored gasps and the white swirls of steam disappeared into the warm air forming a fine mist, a man came up the road that led to the mine. He was tall and his clothes, covered with the red dust of the road, seemed to indicate a farmer rather than a laborer. A sack tied with a leather strap hung from his back and his right hand grasped a thick cane with which he tapped his way forward.

Very soon the stranger reached the platform of the mine, where he asked that he be taken to the overseer. The latter, who at this moment was headed for the shaft, stopped, surprised, before the blind visitor.

"I'm the overseer, my friend," he said. "Who are you and what do you want?"

"My name is Juan Fariña and I want work in the mine," was the brief reply.

All the bystanders looked on and smirked.

"And what can you do?" went on the overseer in a slightly satirical tone.

"I can dig coal," was the tranquil response of the blind man.

A murmur went up from the surrounding group of miners and there burst forth a few ill-suppressed guffaws.

"Comrade," said the overseer contemplating the iron muscles of the job-seeker, "without a doubt, it is not strength that you lack, but to be a coal digger one has to have a good eye and a blind man like you will be no good at it."

"I see nothing," he replied, "but I have good hands and I'm not afraid of any kind of work."

"Then, you're hired," said the boss after a moment's

hesitation. "A blind man who does not beg and wants to work deserves a warm welcome. You can begin when you like."

"I'll be here early tomorrow morning," answered the strange man and he went away, head high, his white pupils fixed on emptiness, through the crowd of workmen who gazed with admiration at his wide shoulders and muscular, athletic body.

On the following morning, Juan Fariña, dressed in the smock and trousers of a miner, a small lunch basket in one hand and his cane in the other, entered the cage with a foreman and several workmen. All wore the traditional leather miners' caps. On the visors of all of these, except that of the blind man, there shone the little lighted oil lamps.

At a sign from the foreman, the cage descended rapidly into the black abyss from which there rose a silght vapor that condensed in crystalline drops on the flexible steel cables.

Once down, they entered the mine following the dark passageways through which the blind man walked with all the sureness of an experienced miner. His companions marveled at the kind of instinct he had for sensing where the obstacles were and avoiding them with astonishing sagacity. His cane was an antenna that moved agilely in all directions, touching the walls, the floor and the ceiling of the slopes, which as they advanced inclined more and more, causing him to lower his great height and to scrape with his back the roughness of the rock.

Soon they left the haulageways and penetrated the mine chambers from which the coal is extracted. In some places, dragging themselves on hands and knees, they crawled along the manways up and down sharp inclines. Everywhere could be heard the incessant pounding: the muffled noise of the pickaxe biting away at the vein mixed with the clearer sound of the sledge hammer against the drill. At times, a violent curse cut through that irrespirable atmosphere impregnated with smoke and coal dust. Deep moans and the continuous pants of tired beasts emerged from those black holes in the darkness where there appeared and disappeared the fugitive lights like will-o'-the-wisps in the lugubrious shadows of the night.

After half an hour of painful progress, they stopped before a small excavation. The vein had been opened in rectangular form; the chamber, very low and narrow, was scarcely a yard high and on its black walls, stabbed by the light of the lamps, the sharp edges of the coal took on bluish, brilliant hues.

After silently listening to the directions of the fore-man, the new miner crawled resolutely into the narrow opening and very soon his labored breathing and dry, repeated blows were added to the muffled sound that already filled the passageways, the working levels and the gloomy corners.

From that day on Fariña became a member of the mine personnel, very soon earning for himself a reputation as an intelligent and courageous workman. However, the deference with which the foremen treated him and his own withdrawn and unsociable character alienated the sympathy of his comrades. They could not understand why the blind man should prefer the work and the misery of a miner to the carefree existence of a beggar. It was not natural and there must be some mystery hidden here.

Intrigued, they watched him carefully, following closely his every step and smallest action. His past was the object of a thorough investigation that produced no results whatsoever. No one knew who he was nor where he came from. As for his blindness, the opinions were divided. There were those who said that those motionless pupils, covered with whitish film, shot phosphorescent sparks into the darkness as do those of a cat and that the blind man was not blind save in the daytime, in the light of the sun.

Others, and there were but few of these, maintained the opposite and to clarify their point they submitted the poor man to the most barbarous proofs. Sometimes it was a coal car turned over right in the middle of his way, or at other times a crossbeam placed at the height of his head against which he bumped violently while invisible wires wrapped themselves round his legs and knocked him down in the slimy black mud of the passage-ways.

Time went on, and more and more the stranger roused the passionate feelings of the souls within the mine. Strange rumors began to circulate about his work. Every day at sunrise he was to be found at the shaft portal ready to descend and he was always the last to ascend to return to his solitary room at the foot of the hill.

During those fifteen hours of gruelling work he tore from the vein more than the minimum requirement of carloads. This disconcerted the more enterprising workers because in that particular place the mineral was harder and the best of them had never been able to reach his record.

This fact strengthened in the credulous imaginations of those simple folk the belief that Fariña was a super-natural being. It was said of him that he went all alone to sleep in the mine and that a partner —whose name they dared not mention— took from the vein the coal necessary to complete the following day's task. And it was no mystery to anyone that at night, when the mine was deserted, there could be heard in the accursed mine chamber a furious drumming that never stopped until dawn. That tireless worker, about whom they now talked in lowered and fearful voices, was no one else but the Devil who wandered day and night in the depths of the mine, hammering mysterious blows in the abandoned workrooms, precipitating rockfalls and opening up through the invisible cracks ways of escape for the treach-erous vapors of firedamp.

Two old miners, night watchmen who guarded the entries, had cautiously approached the place from which proceeded the unusual noise and stopped amazed when they beheld a completely unknown miner at the bottom of the blind man's chamber. He was vigorously attacking the black, brittle block of coal. A spurt of ignited methane that burst from a crack in the wall cast a fiery light about the fantastic figure. In front of him, the coal reflected strange lights and its capricious facets shone like polished jet lit up by the blue flame of the fearful gas.

The witnesses of that infernal scene saw the coal pile up with astounding rapidity before the unknown, nocturnal worker. Suddenly, a piece of coal hacked with great force from the immobile block, dislodged two wooden sustaining timbers from the wall. As they fell against one another, by some strange coincidence they formed on the damp floor of the chamber —a cross.

A terrible blast thundered through the echoing vaults of the mine and a gust of wind struck the faces of the two watchmen who stood nailed to the spot by terror as the hellish vision suddenly vanished.

On the following morning they were both found unconscious at the far end of a badly ventilated tunnel and, from that moment on, no one in the mine doubted that a tenebrous pact linked the hated blind man and the Spirit of Evil. To the dislike which the miners already felt for him, there was now added a superstitious fear. When he went by, they hastily drew away, crossing themselves devoutly. The workers in the chambers near his abandoned their work and transferred to other sections. The loaders refused to take away his coal so that Fariña was obliged, in order not to have to give up his work completely, to be both digger and loader at the same time. Whether it was the excessive work, the overwhelming hardship of which would have broken even the strongest constitution, or whether it was for another unknown cause, the blind man's taciturnity increased from day to day; and, little by little, his muscular body gradually lost that appearance of force and vigor which had contrasted so noticeably with the weak physiques of the miners, those exiles from air and light who wear imprinted upon their waxen faces the longing for fields bathed in sunlight.

It was evident that the blind man was going through a visible decline and the miners who observed him attributed it to the fact that his nefarious pact with the Devil must be drawing to a close. It was an accepted conclusion that an extraordinary event, of which they perhaps would be witnesses, was brewing in the mine. The increasing strangeness of the blind man's conduct gave greater impetus to their suspicions. He was often seen to desert his post and frequent abandoned tunnels. At night he would leave his solitary lodging and wander like a ghost on the seashore. Sometimes, seated on the rocks, he would spend hour after hour listening to the eternal breaking of the waves.

What did he think about in those moments and what secret grief did his soul, closed to all human affection, hide? As to the origin of his blindness, no one ever discovered it.

It was almost the end of his first year in the mine, but the mystery of his life still remained unsolved. Of the various rumors that had circulated about him, there was one that no one mentioned any more. The oldest miners recalled vaguely that, many years before, there had died in the mine a workman, victim of one of the frequent explosions. There had been a sixteen-year-old son with him who had also been dangerously hurt. As a consequence of that accident, the wife and mother lost her reason. The fate of the boy had never been known. Those who remembered all this thought that they saw traces of old burns on Fariña's face. But things never went beyond that and the mystery continued.

From the miners' point of view, the blind man was an enemy to their tranquility and to the very existence of the mine itself. Nothing good could be expected from a man who was in league with the Devil. The alarmists warned of all kinds of evil for the future; and to support their sinister prophecies, they quoted some enigmatic words that the blind man had uttered after a cave-in that cost several miners their lives:

"When I die," he had said mysteriously, "the mine will die with me."

For many that utterance held a menace and for others a prediction of something that would soon come true.

In the week that preceded the great catastrophe, Fariña obtained the job of night watchman for that section of the mine where he worked. It was a job that was relatively easy for him since it involved, mainly, the checking of the ventilation doors.

On the night of the disaster, he presented himself as usual at the portal at the regular hour. It was nine o'clock on the dot when he stepped into the cage and disappeared into the shaft. It was a holiday and the mine was deserted. The weather looked stormy: thick clouds darkened the sky and the north wind, blowing violently high against the hoist, shook the cables and made the wooden structure creak and moan. The sea was agitated and tumultuous and the dashing waves raised their harsh voices along the rocky coast.

The machinist, with one hand on the throttle and the other on the brake, watched attentively the little needle of the indicator. The machine was working at great velocity since its task was reduced to the draining of water from the shafts by means of great buckets which hung under the elevator cages. Right next to the opening, a workman armed with a large iron hook opened the hatches, letting out the water which flowed away down the drainage canal. These two men, and the fireman, who was keeping himself warm in the boiler room, were the only ones on duty at that hour in the mine.

Fariña, meanwhile, had left the elevator and was working his way along the main haulageway, avoiding obstacles with his own peculiar agility. He stopped at the door of the foremen's office, and forcing the lock, he went in. He took from a cabinet against the wall a number of small cylindrical packages which he hid in the pockets of his smock. He hastily grabbed a sack of powder and some rolls of fuses, left the room and went deep into the profundities of the mine.

He walked quickly, sliding noiselessly by the strings of empty cars and soon he left to one side the main arteries and penetrated an abandoned passageway that served only as a ventilation tunnel. This particular place had always been the object of a very special vigilance on the part of the mine engineers. It was situated beneath the sea. Seepage occurred constantly in the tunnel and the possibility of a cave-in was a danger that had worried foremen and operators for many, many years. Here, through the thin layer of sea floor, there penetrated the mysterious mutterings of the ocean and there could be heard distinctly the blades of the boat propellers that beat the waves above, because the tunnel cut obliquely across the main channel into port. Considerable reinforcements had been carried out to avoid having the sea floor break through under water pressure. In the place where seepage was greatest, large, thick beams, which rested on solid legs, formed the collar of the tunnel. Right next to one of these uprights, Fariña stopped. From behind it, he pulled out a rusty carpenter's auger. Six of these uprights were perforated about a yard from the bottom. With the help of the auger, the blind man removed the clay which hid the holes, and, with the calmness and surety of one who is executing an operation that has been meditated for a long time, he introduced into each one of the holes a stick of dynamite with its corresponding fuse. Of these fuses, all of the same size, he made a single string, the end of which he carefully evened off. Then, tying them together with a piece of twine, he poured on top of the thick knot part of the bag of powder. He spilled the rest of the powder in a trickle some yards long across the floor. The main task was finished. The author of that unknown, terrible work straightened himself up and, stretching his arm, he struck a few blows on the damp ceiling with the iron end of his cane, as though he wished to test the thickness of the rock over which flowed the great mobile mass of ocean.

After an instant, he bent down once more. In his right hand shone a lighted match and a stream of sparks ran swiftly across the floor becoming, suddenly, an intense flame that illuminated the farthest reaches of the tunnel. The sinister figure receded then some twenty yards back along the way he had come and stood motionless, with his arms crossed, in the middle of the tunnel. Before him, only a light hissing broke the dead silence. Then, suddenly, a dry crackling reverberated like thunder and one of the uprights, cut in two, flew into splinters beneath the black roof. Seconds later a terrible explosion filled the air and an enormous pile of shattered timbers cut off the tunnel. For a few minutes there could be heard the scraping of rock followed by cave-ins. At first, only small pieces bounced noiselessly on the fallen rubble and then, like the cap of an empty bottle, submerged in deep water, the whole roof of the tunnel blew off at one time. Livid bolts of light swirled a moment in the darkness and something like the gallop of heavy squadrons of cavalry resounded with a fearful din throughout the far corners of the mine.

Outside, the unchained tempest roared with fury and the wind and the sea raised together their irritated voices in a sustained and thundering duet. The machinist on the platform fixed his sleepy gaze on the indicator and on the edge of the shaft where the workman with the iron hook carried out his job, trembling with cold under his soaked clothes. Both thought that they had heard, above the roar of the storm, strange noises that seemed to come from the bottom of the shaft. They also noticed at times that the cables lost their tension as though the weight they supported were being lightened by some unknown force. During those long hours, the two men watched the buckets with anxious eyes in the vain hope that the liquid stream would diminish or stop completely. How far they were from knowing that the water which ran down the mountainside and there joined the sea was but returning to its source!

Toward dawn, the force of the storm abated. The workman near the shaft suddenly heard loud splashes in the drainage canal, as though something were beating about there. He drew near the spot from which the noise came, dumbfounded when he saw an object that seemed to flash as it violently thrashed about near the grating. He quickly took a lantern which hung from a beam of the hoist. His surprise turned into horror! What jumped about there was a live fish, a silver-bellied *corvina*.

Meanwhile the machinist was growing impatient awaiting the expected signals and his imperious shouts could be heard above the wind that was dying down as day approached.

Finally, the absent workman appeared on the platform carrying the squirmy, slimy fish by the tail. The machinist, seeing the object that moved in his hand, cried out from above:

"What's the matter, Juan? What is it?"

"Oh, nothing, just that we're draining the ocean!" was the curt response that struck his ears.

In just a few minutes the alarm whistle sounded out in the mine, for the last time, arousing its sleeping inhabitants. And the steam, that iron organism's very breath of life, abandoned forever its cylinders and boilers and poured itself forth from the open valves in great deafening blasts.

The horrified miners, gathered in groups about the shaft, silently watched the engineers who, with their sounding lines, were testing the extent of the damage. From time to time, there echoed the muted subterranean rumbles of deep cave-ins below. Sea water filled the whole mine and rose through the shaft until it was only fifty yards from the borders of the excavation.

Juan Fariña's name was on everyone's lips. No one doubted for an instant that he was the author of the catastrophe that freed them forever from that prison where for so many generations they had languished midst tortures and unbelievable miseries.

Every year on the anniversary of the terrible accident which destroyed one of the most powerful collieries in the business, the fishermen of those parts say that near the craggy promontory, on the route that the ships take to port, when the first peal of the bells in the tower of a faraway church begins to sound out twelve midnight, there is formed on the salty waves a small, boiling, foaming whirlpool. From its vortex rises the formidable figure of the blind man, with his eyes fixed on the desolate, dead mine.

The fearful apparition disappears with the last vibration of the bells and a foamy stain marks the perilous spot from which the fishing boats, impelled by their frantic rowers, flee in great haste. And woe to the one that dares venture too near that miniature maelstrom; for, attracted by a mysterious force and rudely tossed about by the waves, it will find itself in imminent danger of being sucked down to the depths.

THE DRILL

An old grandfather addressed his open-mouthed young audience and this is the story he told:

Those were the good old days. The gold pieces flowed like water and this dirty paper money of today wasn't even known then.

There were only two mines then —the Chambeque and the Alberto— but the coal was so near the shafts that from each of them many hundreds of tons could be taken each day.

It was at that time that those over at Playa Negra decided to get ahead of us by running a level that went from Playa Blanca right to Santa María. They would thus cut off all the coal to the north of us under the ocean. Scarcely was the news known, when everyone went over to Alto de Lotilla to see the new works that our competitors had hastily begun. They had already constructed a hoist on the very edge of the high tide mark. The rascals wanted to shut us off with as little work as possible. Meanwhile, our foremen didn't just stand around looking on. They tried to find a way to stop this and wore long, startled, pitiful faces.

I had just arrived at the mine one morning when Don Pedro, the head foreman, called me and asked:

"Sebastián, how many miners are there in your gang?"

"Twenty, sir," I replied.

"Choose ten of your best men," he ordered, "and

go with them to Alto de Lotilla. I'll be there in half an hour."

I went below and chose my men. Within the hour we were part of a whole crowd of workmen, carpenters and mechanics gathered on the slope facing the ocean. While the workmen cleared and leveled off with embankments, the carpenters sawed the huge timbers and the mechanics checked the engine which was all ready to go. There was an unearthly din! Every minute miners from Chambeque and Alberto kept coming in. The very choicest of the lot! All between the ages of twenty and twenty-five. Word went round that the chief engineer was going to talk to us. I can still see him, leaning against a pile of wood, giving us a talk that I can remember to this day. After deploring the conduct of the Playa Negra people, who without rhyme nor reason wanted to shut us off, so they could get the underwater coal which we had discovered first and had begun to mine, he said that he counted on our enthusiastic, energetic ability for work to stop that seizure which would be the ruin of us all. Then he explained very briefly what he wanted us to do. In spite of his reserve and the vagueness about certain details, we understood that he intended to sink a shaft in the very place where we were and then open up a level below the ocean, parallel to the beach, that would cut right across the line that the Playa Negra men were heading for. But if we were to be successful, we would have to get there before they did. And here was the difficulty: the distance they had to cover was less than half what we would have to get through to the same point under the ocean.

When the engineer had finished his speech, so great was our enthusiasm, that we shouted for the order to go ahead immediately. We were furious at the Playa Negra men and some proposed a more practical way of solving the question. They wanted to go and throw them down their own shaft, hoist, machinery and all. But the engineer quieted them down saying that violence would only make

the situation worse and put off the difficulty indefinitely.
With calm restored, they proceeded to divide the miners
into twelve squads of ten men each, which would work in
shifts replacing each other every two hours. In this way
the men on the job would always be rested and fresh.

We drew lots for the order of squads and mine
was second. We impatiently waited to relieve the first,
while the ones with the high numbers went home to sleep.

That's what you'd call real work! Bare, with just a
cloth about our loins, we swung those picks with such
frenzy that the earth, clay and stone seemed like some
soft thing into which we dug as easily as the bit of a drill
into soft wood. The sweat ran down us in streams and
we steamed like the blacksmith's iron when he takes it
from the forge and plunges it into water. Some even
fainted; and when the foreman's whistle indicated that
our time was up, a kind of mist blinded us and we could
scarcely stand up on our feet.

In the first week we reached sea level. They put in
great pumps to lower the water and we kept on digging
until another week went by. Suddenly, they ordered us
to stop. The engineers went down with their instruments
and marked the wall with chalk where we were to open
up the level. Without losing a minute, we grabbed our
picks and the work began again with the same fury
as before. We went down agile and refreshed; two hours
later, we came out unrecognizable, exhausted, almost
dead. Up top, the doctor took our pulse, we drank a
little cognac and water and immediately went home to
bed. There were some mishaps. Suddenly someone
would fall down on all fours and just stay there without
moving. Others would be attacked by nose bleeds and
the blood would run from their noses and ears. They
would be replaced immediately from the reserve squad
and the work went on day and night without a minute's,
not even a second's, pause.

It was impossible to do more but the foremen still
thought it too little. They acted as though something

were eating them. And no wonder, for we were digging from north to south, to shut off the Playa Negra diggers who were headed east and we had double the distance to go. We'd been working for a month when, one morning, the engineers came to survey the level again. This delayed us a lot. They talked and measured and re-measured. Then, suddenly, they ordered us to stop work until further notice. As we were all dying of curiosity and wanted to know whether we had lost or won, no one wanted to leave the mine until we found out what was going on. As foreman of my squad, I accosted Don Pedro, the chief overseer, who had his ear to the wall and I asked:

"Have we caught up with them yet?"

He motioned me to keep quiet and then I, too, put my ear to the wall. I listened with all my might and suddenly I seemed to hear, far away, some little knocks as though someone were tapping on the stone. I listened carefully and, when I was absolutely sure, I called the overseer and said:

"Don Pedro, this is where they are drilling."

He came over and we listened together. Suddenly in the lamplight I saw his eyes glisten. The blows of the hammer on the drill were becoming more and more audible. At that moment the engineers arrived; and after listening, too, with their ears glued to the wall, they unrolled a blueprint and began to work with their instruments. Then they chalked a large cross on the wall, gave some orders to the overseer and left as pleased as punch. They had scarcely gone, when a dozen or more carpenters appeared. Hastily they set up a door that closed off a space about ten yards long at the end of the tunnel. When the door had been hung and all its cracks had been thoroughly calked, the carpenters withdrew. Only the overseers and the squad foremen remained listening to the sound of the drill that kept drawing closer. However, several hours went by and it must have been about three in the afternoon when the overseer said:

"Go up and tell them to get the brazier ready!"

I hurried and when I got back the sound of the drill was so clear that I calculated it wouldn't be more than half an hour before it came through the wall. The tunnel was six feet high here and cut through a strata of blue tuff that didn't let through a single drop of water, even though the ocean was over our heads. While we waited silently, we never ceased wondering at and admiring the engineers' exact calculations. We didn't know, yet, that taking advantage of the negligence of the Playa Negra overseers, two of our men had gone into the enemy's mine and taken down the level and direction of their cut.

Just as I had calculated, not half an hour had gone by when the first bits of tuff began falling from the wall, about five feet from the floor. We all knew what this meant and anxiously waited for the drill point to break through the wall so that we could knock it off with one good blow. We'd make our enemies see that they had lost and that we were the masters down there under the sea! Hammer in hand, we were waiting for the opportune moment, when Don Pedro made us a sign to get out of the way. Pushing his left shoulder against the wall he spit into his hands, rubbed them together and then stood, eyes glued to the tuff that was swelling out like a blister.

I shall never forget that moment. We all had our eyes fixed on the overseer, who was like one of those fairy tale giants. Six feet tall, his massive body, assuming enormous proportions in the light, seemed to fill the whole space. His strength was well-known in the whole mine. I have often seen him, in jest, lift a man in each hand and hold them up in the air as though they were newborn babes.

One foot ahead of the other, head slightly bowed, he was waiting for that instant when the drill would come through the wall. He didn't have long to wait. With each blow, the tuff fell in larger and larger pieces until, suddenly, something shiny came through the wall knocking out a thick plank. Quick as a lightning bolt, the overseer grabbed it and we heard his bones cracking. He straightened up, stood quiet, fixed against the wall, head thrown back and puffing like the bellows of a forge. Our eyes could barely take in what they saw! The end of the drill stuck out of the wall about fifty centimetres, bent over like an angle iron and it moved from side like the pendulum of a clock.

The grandfather paused, and after taking in his trembling old fingers the lighted cigarette that one of his attentive listeners held out to him, he went on:

There is very little left to tell. The Playa Negra miners, who couldn't even remotely guess what was happening, attributed the accident to a simple obstruction in the way of their drill. While they made every effort imaginable to loosen it, widening the hole, we had placed in front of it a brazier full of burning coals. Then the overseer ordered the men to abandon the mine. That left the two of us to finish the job. All was ready in a minute.

After trying the door to make sure it was firmly secured, I prudently drew away. Don Pedro took in his arms, as though it were light as a feather, an enormous sack of chili which had just been brought down. From the doorway he threw it onto the burning coals. Without stopping, he kicked the door shut and turning ran to the exit shaft. I was ahead of him and reached the elevator first. Even though they took us right up, we felt a horrible burning in our throats that caused an unbearable dry cough.

Not ten minutes later, we saw that something extraordinary was happening at the other mine. The alarm bell went off and something very serious indeed must have happened below because the pealing of the bell was desperate. As we were higher than they, we could

[80]

see everything that went on. When the elevator came
up, the mouth of the shaft was crowded with people.
Those who came up were besieged with questions:
"What's the matter? What has happened?" But the poor
devils couldn't answer. A strange cough shook them from
head to foot. Then we all broke into shouts and hurrahs
that those of Playa Negra answered with insults and
curses.

Well, to finish my story, I only need to say that every
attempt our enemies made to go down into the mine and
take up their work again was futile. Days, weeks, even
months went by and it was still useless. Scarcely did the
elevator go down a few yards into the shaft when they
yelled to be brought up immediately and they came out
half-choked to death, coughing desperately.

A better stratagem could never have been devised.
The chili smoke, closed in at the end of our tunnel,
escaped so gradually through the orifice of the drill, that
it threatened never to end. And then the inevitable happened. The timber reinforcements, but lightly put in, gave
way and let in the sea water.

Just six months later, the famous mine of Playa Negra was only a saltwater pond that the sand of the dunes
slowly began to fill.

THE SHOTGUN

While Petaca kept vigil at the door, Cañuela, perched on the table, took down from the mantel the heavy, rusty, old shotgun.

The cheerful rays of the sun, filtering in through all the cracks in the old farmhouse, filled the interior with dazzling light. The two boys were alone that morning. Cañuela's old grandparents, Pedro and Rosalia, had left early that morning for the village after telling their grandson to be a good boy while they were gone.

In spite of his limited strength —Cañuela was only nine and skinny as a rail —he managed to get down the gun. Seated on the edge of the bed, with the barrel between his legs and the butt steadied against the floor, he examined the terrible instrument with great serious-ness and in minute detail. With his blonde,sun-bleached hair and clear blue, innocent, eyes he formed a direct contrast to his cousin, Petaca, with his black, thick hair and lively dark eyes. Petaca was two years his senior and ruled Cañuela with an iron hand.

They had had a hunting project on for some time now, which had been the subject for innumerable secret meetings and consultations. But they had encountered one obstacle after another to their plans. How were they to get powder, shot and percussion caps? Finally, one afternoon, when Cañuela sat before the fire watching the supper pot, he suddenly saw in the doorway Petaca's silent, furtive figure. When Petaca realized that the old folks were not at home, from under his clothes, before Cañuela's astonished eyes, he drew forth a big sack of powder.

About a league away from the farm was a quarry which provided the surrounding villages with building materials. Petaca's father was the boss there. Every morning, from a deep hole in the rock, he brought out the day's supply of powder. The boy had tried every trick he knew to get one of those bags which his father kept with him in the small tent from which he directed the work. Every one of his schemes and stratagems had failed lamentably under his father's vigilant eyes. Finally, desperately anxious to get what he wanted, he tried an heroic measure. He had observed that when a blast was ready to go off, and the signal given, all the men, even the boss, sought shelter in a hole cut for that purpose in the side of the mountain and that they never came out until the explosion was over. One morning, dragging himself forward like a snake, he hid near the tent. Soon, three blows on a steel bar announced that the wick had been lighted. He saw his father and all the quarrymen run to hide in the cave.

This was the moment. Rushing over to the pile of sacks, he grabbed one, then ran as fast as his legs would carry him, jumping like a little goat over the rock piles that covered a large area down the mountainside. The explosion shook the ground under his feet. Enormous projectiles zoomed about his ears and the rocks fell like hail all about him. But he was not hit and by the time the quarrymen emerged from their hiding place, Petaca was far away, jubilantly pressing his glorious prize to his panting breast.

That afternoon, a Thursday, the boys agreed that the hunting expedition would take place the following Sunday, normally a free day for them because that was when the grandparents took their poultry and vegetables to market. Until then, they would have to hide the powder. Many hiding places were suggested, then rejected. Cañuela proposed that they should dig a hole in a corner of the orchard and hide it there, but his cousin dissuaded him. He knew a boy who had done just that and, days later, he had found nothing but the sack. All the contents had been destroyed by the dampness. Therefore they must look for a good dry place. Cañuela, the stupid one, who according to Petaca never had a bright idea, suddenly pointed to the fireplace:

"Let's bury it in the ashes."

Petaca looked at him in astonishment. Usually, all his little blond cousin had to do was propose something for him to oppose it. This time, however, he was ready to accept the suggestion. But a look at the fire stopped him. Suppose it caught fire, he thought. Suddenly he jumped with joy. He had found the solution. In an instant, both boys had swept away the embers and the ashes and into the hearth they dug a hole about forty centimetres deep. In this they placed the sack of powder, replaced the dirt and put back the coals and the clay pot that had been cooking there.

Half an hour and all was nicely done. Petaca left with the promise that he would have the shot and the percussion caps before Sunday.

In the days that followed, Cañuela kept wondering about a possible explosion. But the only thing that really bothered him was the possible loss of the pot of food, which would leave him and his grandparents supperless. This sinister thought would grow stronger when he saw his grandmother, cheeks puffed, blowing with all her might to liven the coals. Little did she know that there before her very nose was a Vesuvius ready at any moment to erupt. When this happened, Cañuela would tiptoe to the door with a sidelong glance, muttering anxiously:

"Caramba, now it will surely explode!"

But it didn't and the boy soon lost all fear.

When, on Sunday, the old folks, with their loads on their backs, had disappeared in the distance down the mountain path, the two children, radiant with joy, began their preparations for the long-awaited expedition. Petaca had kept his word. He had stolen a box of percussion caps from his father and the shot had been very economically supplied in the form of tiny pebbles taken from the stream bed.

Once they had dug up the powder, which they found perfectly dry and warm to the touch, and inspected the old gun, which was as venerable and ancient as its owner, there was nothing left to do, after securely fastening the door behind them, but to set out across the hills and the stubble.

In front, gun on shoulder, marched Petaca. Close behind followed Cañuela, his ample pants pockets filled with the munitions of war. They argued over the way they should go. Cañuela thought they should go down the ravine and follow it to the valley where they would find flocks of *tencas* and thrush. But his stubborn cousin wanted to go through the stubble where the *loicas* and the partridges abounded.

Petaca wore a castoff jacket of his father, the sleeves of which had been shortened and the bottom cut off above the pockets, so that he lacked these very useful articles. Cañuela, on the other hand, had no jacket, only a shirt, but he sported a pair of thick cloth pants that had enormous pockets that were his pride and joy, a storage chest, pantry and arsenal all in one.

Petaca perspired and puffed under the weight of the unwieldy gun. Standing erect, he tried to hold the pose befitting a hunter and he stubbornly refused to listen to Cañuela's pleas that he relinquish the precious instrument even for a little while.

In the beginning, Cañuela, filled with the ardor of the hunt, wanted to fire on every living thing they saw, even the swarms of mosquitoes that buzzed in the air. Every minute or so he called his cousin with a soft "Pst, pst." When Petaca turned questioningly, Cañuela, eyes sparkling, would point to a miserable little *chincol* hopping along in the grass. Then the mighty

Nimrod would shrug his shoulders disdainfully and continue his triumphal march across the hills, bent low by
the gun which was so much taller than he.

Finally, the exigent hunter saw before him game
worth the honor of a shot. It was a male *loica* with a
blood-red breast. It was singing, merrily perched on a
hedgerow. The boys threw themselves down, then crawled
like snakes through the underbrush. The bird calmly watched their movements without the least bit of fear
until they were four steps away. Then he opened his
wings, flew and lighted on the grass fifty yards away.
The chase was on! Petaca would get near enough to
cock his gun. The bird with a mocking, challenging cry
would fly another hundred paces. As though to try his
enemies, he flew over the roughest spots but always
kept in view of his pursuers. After some hours of this,
they were bathed in perspiration, all scratched and their
clothes were torn to shreds. Not a bit discouraged, they
hunted their prey with savage enthusiasm. Finally, the
bird, tired of such persistent persecution, rose into the air
and, flying over a deep ravine, disappeared into the
woods of the opposite slope.

At this point, Cañuela and Petaca were crawling
along a furrow on all fours. They stood up, looked at
each other and then, without a word, kept right on,
resolved that they would drop dead before they would
give up such a prize.

After the exhausting trip through the ravine, the
first thing they saw on the other side was the fugitive,
perched on a small bush, tearing the tender stems with
his strong bill. No sooner did they catch sight of him
than down they dropped. Petaca, his sparkling eyes fixed
on the bird, began to crawl on his stomach, dragging
the gun with him. He scarcely drew a breath. He put
all his heart and soul into that silent approach. Four
yards from the tree, he stopped, and with a mighty effort, he hoisted the gun into place. But the very second

that he was going to pull the trigger, Cañuela, who had
followed without even being noticed, suddenly cried out
in his penetrating, clarion-like voice:

"Hey, wait, it isn't loaded!"

The bird flapped its wings and then disappeared
like an arrow toward the horizon.

Petaca jumped up and, leaping on the little blond,
he beat him up. "You beast, you dumbbell! You've chased
away the bird the very minute he was going to fall
dead. My aim was perfect."

When Cañuela, sobbing, stammered, "But I told
you that it wasn't loaded!" Petaca, hands on hips, eyes
flaming with rage, answered, "Why didn't you wait for
the shot to come out?"

Cañuela, completely taken aback, stopped crying,
wiped his eyes on the back of his hand and stood looking
at Petaca with his mouth open. Of course! Why hadn't
he thoughs of that! He deserved those punches. He really was a stupid goose!

So they were friends again. Stretched out in the
shade of a tree, they rested awhile. They were so tired.
Petaca, over his fury, felt a little remorseful because,
in truth, it wasn't very clear, even to him, how he could
have killed the bird with an unloaded gun, no matter how
good his aim. But to confess this would have meant proving his little cousin right, so he kept his reflections to
himself. He would have given anything to have killed
that bird that had led them such a merry chase. If only
they had loaded the gun when they started out. But
there was still time to repair that major omission. He
called Cañuela to help him with the serious and delicate
operation. Neither one had the slightest idea of how
to go about it for they had never seen anyone load a
gun. Cañuela stood up on a tree trunk so he could look
into the gun which Petaca held upright. Ramrod in hand,
he awaited orders. But here was the first difficulty.
What went in first? The powder or the pebbles?

Petaca, although he was quite puzzled, was inclined to believe that it was the powder and he was going to do it that way, when Cañuela timidly expressed the same idea. Always contrary, Petaca, of course, inmediately refused to accept Cañuela's opinion. It was enough that his cousin just mention something for Petaca to do exactly the opposite. He scoffed at such an idea. You'd have to be stupid as an ox to think of such a thing.

It would have to be the other way, first shot, then powder. Cañuela did not even venture a reply. He had no desire for further proof from Petaca backed by another beating. He dropped a handful of pebbles into the barrel, then two big fistfuls of powder. A bunch of dry grass served as a wad and with the percussion cap all set nicely by Petaca, the gun was ready to fire its deadly charge. Hoisting it to his shoulder, the intrepid little hunter, followed by Cañuela, set forth again anxiously scrutinizing the horizon for signs of a victim. There were lots of birds but they took to flight the minute the end of the gun threatened to knock them from their perch. Not one had the decency to wait quietly while the hunter aimed and re-aimed a thousand times! Finally, a dauntless *chincol,* preening its feathers on a branch, had the good grace to wait unti Petaca had finished all his strange and complicated manipulations. Kneeling in the grass, with gun supported on a tree trunk, Petaca aimed while Cañuela, at his shoulder, held both hands over his ears to shut out the noise that he imagined would be awful. Petaca, too, remembering the sound of the explosions in the quarry, hesitated before he pulled the trigger. But the thought that his cousin might make fun of his cowardice made him turn his head, shut his eyes and fire.

To his surprise, instead of the bang he expected, all he heard was a most unexciting little dry, sharp crack. How can such a big shotgun make such a little noise, he thought. He searched quickly for the bird and not seeing it on the branch let out a whoop of joy, expecting to find it on the ground, feet up.

Cañuela, who had seen the *chincol* calmly fly away, did not dare to disillusion him. In fact, Petaca so enthusiastically exclaimed over his good aim and how he had seen the feathers flying through the air, and the bird fall crushed to the ground, that he completely convinced Cañuela, who forgot what he had seen. So they both diligently searched the underbrush until, worn out, they finally had to give up. But both had now smelled the gunpowder. Their enthusiasm had mounted. It was becoming a thirst for extermination and destruction that nothing could assuage.

They rapidly loaded the gun, and having lost all fear of it, they ardently pursued their imaginary massacre. Their illusion was maintained by the slight little explosion that the cap made. They had, of course, noticed that the powder did not smoke very much, but soon they forgot even that.

Only one thing clouded their joy. They could not get a single bird no matter how much Petaca swore that he had seen one fall dead as a door nail with all his feathers almost plucked out by the grape shot of the pebbles. That was for Cañuela's benefit, but he began to believe deep down that there was something wrong with the darned powder. He remembered how a twisted arrow curved and did not hit its mark. So he promised himself not to close his eyes next time nor to turn his head away but watch the direction of the shot. However, an unexpected catastrophe stopped him from ever making the experiment.

Cañuela, up on a tree trunk, after he had just put in a great big fistful of pebbles, cried out in alarm:

"The shotgun's ruined!"

Petaca looked in surprise at the gun, then at his cousin, puzzled as to the meaning of those words. Cañuela pointed to the barrel, where the last bit of wadding still stuck out. Petaca lowered the gun to feel the mouth of the barrel with his fingers. But he knew there wasn't room to put in one more grain of powder or anything else. He frowned. Now he knew why the old gun had become so heavy.

They had been heading toward home as the afternoon advanced. Mulling over in his mind the probable consequences of this affair, Petaca decided, after a while, to escape himself and leave Cañuela to face the music. Too well did he know his grandfather's temper to risk getting within his reach.

But suddenly, his fertile imagination discovered such a wonderful solution that he gave up the idea of escaping. He planted himself in front of his cousin who, up to now, had not dared to open his mouth. Whatever he so enthusiastically explained to him must not have met with Cañuela's approval, because, with tears in his eyes, he tried to oppose him. But, as usual, he ended up by giving in and both boys began to gather dry leaves and branches, which they piled on the ground. When they figured they had enough, Cañuela drew from his bottomless pockets a box of matches and lit the pile. Petaca picked up the gun, placed it on the bonfire, then both hastily withdrew. From a distance, they watched the progress of the fire. Petaca was just about to go near it to add more fuel, when a formidable crash deafened them. The bonfire went flying in all directions and sinister whistlings cut through the air.

When the first tremendous shock was over, they looked at each other. Petaca was as pale as his cousin, but his energetic nature made him come to sooner. He walked over to the site of the explosion. It was as clean as if it had been newly raked. He looked and looked, but not a trace of the gun did he find. Cañuela, who had followed him, crying his head off, suddenly stopped, petrified with terror. Up on the hill, thirty paces away, advancing upon them with great long strides, was the tall figure of their grandfather. He was furious. He gesticulated, shouting, his right arm high, brandishing a smoking firebrand that looked suspiciously like the stock of a shotgun.

Petaca, who had seen the aparition at the same time as his cousin, ran down the hillside, slapping his legs with the palms of his hands and whistling his favorite tune. As he ran he searched the ground, thinking that, as his grandfather had found the stock, so he might come upon the barrel or at least some little pieces out of which he could make a blunderbuss. Then he could discharge salutes or kill ducks in the lagoon.

THE TOWLINE

Believe me, it is difficult for me to tell these things.
In spite of all the years that have gone by, the memory
is still painful.

While the narrator, lost in his own thoughts, silently went over
the memory in his own mind, there was a profound silence in the little
cabin of the brigantine, called "The Dolphin." Had it not been for the
slight swinging of the lamp that hung from the blackened ceiling, we
would have believed ourselves on dry land—far from "The Dolphin,"
which lay anchored a mile off the coast.
Suddenly, the mariner took his pipe from his mouth and his
serious, slow voice resounded as he began his story:

I was only a boy then and served as cabin boy and
apprentice aboard the "St. George," a little tug out of
Lota.

The crew consisted of the captain, the pilot, the engineer, the fireman and myself, the youngest of them
all. Never has a boat had such a united crew as did that
much loved "St. George." We were like one big, happy
family; the captain was the father and the rest of us,
his sons. And what a man he was! How we all loved
him! More than love, it was idolatry! Strong and just,
he was kindness itself. He always took the most difficult
job for himself, helping everyone else with his and
never ever lost his good humor. Oftentimes, seeing that
my many tasks had worn me to exhaustion, he would
cheerfully and affectionately take over, saying: "Come

now, lad, rest a bit while I stretch the kinks out of my own muscles."

When, from under the awning, protected from the sun or the rain, I looked out on his great broad figure, his red face with its blond graying moustache and his blue eyes that were as frank and open as those of a child, my whole mind and soul would flood with such profound love for him, that to save him from peril I would have sacrificed my life without a moment's hesitation.

The narrator paused for a minute to raise the pipe to his lips and, after a big puff, he went on:

One day we weighed anchor at dawn and headed for Santa Maria. We had in tow a barge full of lumber on which we were going to bring back a cargo of seal skins that were to be loaded the following morning onto the transatlantic steamer that was on its way to the Straits. The sea was as smooth as glass, the sky blue and the air so clear we could see every detail of the Gulf of Arauco.

Everybody aboard the "St. George" was happy, but the happiest of all was the captain, for the skipper of the barge that we were towing was no other than his own son Marcos. Standing in the stern, Marcos held the long tiller in his hands as though it were a reed, making that great hulk follow in the wake that the tug's propellers were cutting in the blue waves.

An only son, Marcos, was also our friend, a happy and likeable companion. Never was the saying, "like father, like son," more definitely proved than with these two. They were alike physically and morally; the son was a living picture of his father. I was twenty-one at the time and he was only two years older than I.

It was a delightful crossing. We skirted the island to the south of us and by noon we had reached the cove which was the end of our journey. After the hard and laborious job of unloading the barge, we waited for the new shipment which, for some unforeseen reason, wasn't ready. This displeased the captain and with good cause. The weather, so beautiful that morning, changed suddenly as afternoon came on. A northeaster, that got colder by the minute, was whipping up the sea in violent gusts. Outside the inlet, the waves were whirling high in foamy spirals. The slate-gray sky, covered over with scudding clouds that shut off the horizon, looked menacing. Soon the rain began to fall. Heavy downpours obliged us to seek shelter under our oilskins while we discussed the unseasonable squall. Although the morning's calm ocean and the clear atmosphere had made us fear a change in weather, we were in no way prepared for this kind of storm. If it hand'nt been for the need to meet that transatlantic liner and the peremptory orders we had received about it, we would have stayed in the shelter of the cove until the violence of the storm abated.

Finally the delayed cargo appeared and we proceeded to load it in all haste. Although we worked like mad to hurry it up, it was nightfall when we finished. We immediately left the harbor with the barge in tow. In its stern and on its seats, through the rain and the foam that the wild wind was snatching up from the crests of the waves, we could just make out the silhouettes of Marcos and his four oarsmen.

Everything went well at first while we were in the lee of the high shore, but all this changed completely as soon as we entered the channel that led to the Gulf.

A sheet of rain and hail hit us on the bow and carried away the canvas awning that, grazing my head, swept over like the wings of a gigantic stormy petrel, the winged harbinger of trouble.

At a word from the captain who was clinging to the wheel, the pilot and I ran to batten down the cabin and engine-room hatches. We spread over them the thick, waterproof canvas covers and secured them tightly.

I had scarcely reached my post by the chock when a whitish light shone by the bow and a mass of water burst against my legs. Holding desperately to the rail, I resisted the impact of that wave which was followed by two more just a few seconds apart. For an instant, I thought all was over but the captain's voice, shouting through the megaphone —"Full steam ahead!"— made me realize that we were still afloat.

The whole hull of the "St. George" shook and creaked. The propeller had doubled its revolutions and the strident squeaking of the tow cable told us that we were moving a lot faster. For what to me seemed a long time, the situation remained the same. Although it was still extremely rough, we hadn't shipped water again as we had at the exit of the channel. The "St. George," at full speed, bravely maintained the course marked for us by the beams from the lighthouse high on the promontory overlooking the port entrance.

But this moment of relative calm —this truce between wind and sea— suddenly ceased when, according to our calculations, we were about half way across the Gulf. This time, the fury of the unchained elements reached such proportions that no one aboard the "St. George" doubted for one minute what the outcome of this crossing would be.

The captain and the pilot, holding onto the wheel with all their strength, were keeping the course, running with the northeaster that threatened to become a hurricane. The constant flashes of lightning showed us that the furious waves were increasing in intensity, pounding our little boat that righted after each lurch with a great deal of difficulty. We were navigating between the waves and the danger of capsizing became more and more imminent.

Suddenly, above the din of the storm, the captain's voice reached my ears: "Antonio, watch out for the towline!"

"Aye, aye, sir," I answered but a furious gust drowned out my words. The lantern, fastened to the funnel, threw out only feeble rays over the deck of the "St. George." The silhouettes of the captain and the pilot were just vaguely discernible. All the rest of the boat, from stem to stern, was submerged in deep shadow.

Of the barge, separated from the tug by twenty fathoms, the full length of the hawser, all that could be seen was the pale phosphorescence which the waves give off as they hit an obstacle in the dark. But the creaking of the taut cable clearly indicated that the barge still followed in our wake. Although we could not see it, we felt it there, very close to us, wrapped in the midnight darkness that grew denser every minute.

All of a sudden, above the deafening roar of the storm, I thought I heard a muffled, persistent sound to starboard. The captain and the pilot must have noticed it too, because by the light of the lantern I saw them turn to the right and stand still, listening very attentively to the strange noise. A few minutes went by and those muted thuds that sounded like distant thunder were getting louder and louder, until they reached a point which allowed for no possible doubt. The "St. George" was drifting toward the shoals of Punta de Lavapié.

The crashing of the waves on the feared and perilous shoals soon drowned out with their resounding, terrifying roar all the other voices of the storm.

I didn't know what my companions thought, but an idea suddenly struck me and I said to myself fearfully:

"The towline is our destruction!"

At that precise instant, a vivid bolt of lightning cut through the blackness and with one voice from both boats came the anguished cry:

"The shoals! The shoals!"

Each man had seen outlined in the flash of lightning the whitish surface dotted with black spots only three or four cable lengths to starboard of the "St. George." It was useless to discuss how we had gotten there. We all knew perfectly well what had happened. The great open surface that the half-loaded barge exposed to the wind not only slowed up the progress of the tug; it almost kept us from moving at all. Since we had left the channel, we had scarcely advanced a bit and had been dragged by the current to the shoals that we thought were miles away. The propeller turned in vain. The force of the wind was stronger than the engine and we were drifting slowly toward the rocks that filled our hearts with terror. There was only one thing that could save us. Cut the towline immediately and abandon the barge. If we veered round to get near Marcos and his companions, we would inevitably founder as the waves caught our flank. The captain's dilemma was terrible: either we would all die or he could save his boat sending his son to a horrible death. The thought of it upset me so that I forgot my own troubles and imagined only the terrible struggle that must be going on in the captain's affectionate and loving heart.

From my post I could make out his broad figure in the feeble lamp rays. Glued to the railing, I tried to figure out from his attitude whether he had found any other alternative ways of saving us.

Supposing that an audacious manoeuvre, or unexpected help, or the sudden abatement of the northeaster were to end our plight happily! But, any manoeuvre, excepting that of keeping our bow to the wind, was pure folly. Out of that blackness no help could come. And there wasn't the slightest hope that the storm would let up, none at all. On the contrary, its fury seemed to be increasing. The rumbling thunder accompanied the howl of the crashing waves and the lightning, ripping through the clouds, threatened to set the heavens on fire. In the blinding light of the flashes the shoals seemed to be coming up to meet us. A few minutes more and the

"St. George" and the barge would be broken to bits on that mad whirlpool.

Above the deafening roar, the thundering voice of the captain came through the megaphone:

"More steam!"

A muffled vibration told me a moment later that the order had been carried out. The propeller was whirling round madly; the hull groaned as if it were going to fall apart. I saw the captain turn around and guessed his infinite desperation when all his efforts only held off the catastrophe a few short moments.

The engine-room hatch was suddenly raised and through the hole appeared the engineer's head. A gust blew off his cap and his white hair blew all about his forehead. Holding grimly to the guard rail, he stood still while a dazzling flash lit up the darkness. One look was enough and raising his voice above that infernal confusion, he shouted:

"Captain, we're going to hit the shoals!"

If the captain answered, I didn't hear it. A minute of waiting that seemed endless went by, a minute which the engineer spent, no doubt, trying to find a way to avoid the imminent disaster. But the result must have been frightening, for under the lantern I saw his face take on an expression of unspeakable terror as he fixed his eyes on his old shipmate. The captain, overcome by this conflict between his father love and his duty to save the ship trusted to his care, stood there by the helm, in a state of shock, crazed with grief.

Some seconds went by. The engineer advanced a few steps along the rail and began to speak to the captain, raising his voice energetically. But such was the noise of the storm that only a vague word here and there reached me: "resignation... the will of God... honor... duty."

The only thing I heard completely were his final words:

"My life doesn't matter, Captain, but you can't let these other lads die."

The engineer referred to me, the pilot and the fireman whose head popped up every now and then from the hatchway.

I never knew whether the captain answered his old friend's appeal for just then, to the swishing of the waves that swept the boat, was added a violent clap of thunder. I was sure my last hour had come. At any moment now we were going to hit bottom. I began to stammer a prayer when out of the darkness astern I recognized Marcos's voice. Although they were very weak, I heard the words distinctly:

"Father, cut the cable. Hurry! Hurry!"

A cold chill went up and down my spine. We were at the end of our struggle, about to run aground and be swallowed up by the boiling maelstrom. What a great hero Marcos seemed to me! The fortitude he demonstrated in that crisis brought tears to my eyes. What a courageous friend, and now we would never see each other again.

The "St. George," assaulted by the furious waves, began to dance an infernal saraband. Like a little cur held in the jaws of a great mastiff, she was shaken from stem to stern and from port to starboard with a formidable violence. When her propeller was out of the water she creaked as though she were about to fall into a million pieces. Blinded by the torrential rain, I was hanging on to the chock when the stentorian voice of the engineer hit me like a bolt:

"Antonio, get the axe!"

I turned toward the wheel and a confused mass struggling there brought me out of my stupor. The captain and the engineer were battling it out on the deck. Then I saw the engineer, who had thrown off his adversary, hurtling towards the stern, exclaiming:

"Antonio, cut the cable! Lively, lad!"

Almost without thinking, I leaned over, raised the cover of the tool box, grabbed the axe by the handle, but just as I was about to chop the cable, with my arm raised high, the lightning flashed and revealed my intent to the men on the barge. I heard an enraged shriek:

"They're cutting the cable! They're cutting the cable! Damned assassins! No! No!"

Meanwhile, aroused by the cries and wanting to be done with this once and for all, I slashed at the cable, until, all at once, something like a tentacle wrapped itself around my legs and threw me down on all fours. I stood up just as the engineer shouted to the pilot:

"Head for the lighthouse!"

I looked for the captain and just made out his silhouette by the chock. It only took him a second to discover the severed cable. Letting out a heart-rending cry, he leaned out over the gunwale, balanced there in space crying: "Marcos! Marcos!" I grabbed his leg in the nick of time, dragging him back from that abyss. We rolled together over the dark deck in a desperate struggle. We fought in silence, he to free himself, and I to keep him quiet. In other circumstances, the captain would have had the advantage, but he was wounded and the loss of blood was making him weak. In the fight with the engineer, his head must have struck some iron object because several times when our faces touched I thought I felt a warm liquid running down from his hair. Suddenly he stopped fighting. We stood with our back to the gunwale without moving. Then he began to moan:

"Antonio, my son, let me go to join Marcos!"

I burst into tears, but he, getting more and more excited, cried:

"You fiend! I saw you chop the cable. But it wasn't the cable you cut, do you hear, not the cable. It was his neck, his neck, you executioner! Your hands are all stained with blood. Take them off me, don't touch me, murderer!"

I heard his teeth grind and then, emitting ferocious howls, he leaped on me:

"Now it's your turn. Over you go!"

Madness had given the captain new strength. Tripping me, he picked me up and lifted me into the air like a straw. I beheld the vision of a fatal and inevitable death; but at that very instant a wave hit the bow and poured down to the stern like an avalanche, knocking us over and dragging us along the deck. As I fell, my hands hit something hard and round and I held on for dear life. When the wave had passed, I found myself hanging on with both hands to the severed piece of towline. As for the captain, he had disappeared.

At that moment, aboard "The Dolphin," the pilot opened the cabin door.

"Captain," he said, "it's full tide. Do we weigh anchor?"

The captain nodded his assent and we all stood up. It was time to go ashore and as we neared the ladder to go down to the longboat, our friend concluded:

The rest of the story isn't very interesting. The "St. George" was saved. The next day I shipped as cabin boy aboard this boat, "The Dolphin." That was fifteen years ago... Now, I'm its captain.

INAMIBLE

Rupert Tapia, alias "The Rat," was an officer of the third rank on the county police force, and that morning, while on duty in town, he strutted back and forth in the middle of the street with the stiff, solemn air of a functionary who is quite aware of the importance of his job.

At thirty-five, officer Tapia was a fat, healthy man of average height, and greatly admired by his cronies. He was considered a fount of knowledge, because he not only had all the police ordinances and bylaws at the tip of his tongue, but was also familiar with the relevant articles of the Penal Code. His deep, sonorous voice, his long, flowery speeches, and the studied dignity of his manner helped strengthen his reputation. But of all his talents the most characteristic was the uncanny knack he had of inventing a word whenever the precise one had slipped his mind. And so striking were his creations, that even after hearing them only once, it was impossible to forget them.

As "The Rat" walked on, his nail-studded shoes resounded on the cobblestones, and his swarthy face reflected a certain dissatisfaction. He had been assigned to a district where there were few pedestrians and little traffic. The water from the drains collected at the foot of the tree-lined streets, and since there were few passersby, it would be almost impossible to make an arrest, even for the most trifling infraction.

And this irked him, because for some time now he had been aspiring to wear a sergeant's gold chevrons, and had determined to prove to his superiors how zealous he was in the performance of his duties. Suddenly he heard a scream, followed by peals of laughter. He turned about and less than half a block away he spotted a girl of about sixteen or seventeen running on the sidewalk, hotly pursued by a youth with a small whip-like object in his right hand. "The Rat" knew them both. The girl was a maidservant in the corner house, and the youth was Martin, the carriage driver, who had just come from the outskirts of town where he went every morning to set his horses out to pasture. The girl ran on, giggling and screeching, and fled inside the house. Her pursuer lingered a moment in the doorway, and then approached the policeman, smiling.

"That wench sure can scream," he said. "And imagine, I didn't even get a chance to touch the nape of her neck with it."

And lifting his hand, he displayed a small snake which he was holding by the tail.

"It's dead. I caught it at the foot of the hill when I left the horses. If you want me to, I'll leave it with you so you can have some fun scaring all the women that come along."

But instead of taking the snake Martin offered him, "The Rat" let his heavy hand fall on the carriage driver's shoulders.

"Come along now," he boomed. "We're going to headquarters."

"Me? What for? Are you arresting me?" the practical joker of a few minutes earlier protested, now flushed with surprise and indignation.

And in the solemn tone he always adopted at times like this, Officer Tapia pointed to the snake and said:

"I'm taking you in because you've been fooling around with animals."

At this point he hesitated a moment, and then, with great emphasis, added:

"Because you've been fooling on the public thoroughfare with *inamible* animals."

By now the young man had disposed of the *corpus delicti* by throwing it in the muddy drainwater, yet despite his protests, the policeman would not let him go.

At headquarters, the officer of the guard who was napping at the desk gave them a very cold reception. The evening before he had attended a baptismal dinner, and a generous supply of alcohol plus a lack of sleep had combined to dull his brain and muddle his ideas. His head was buzzing like the proverbial pot full of crickets.

After yawning and fidgeting about in his chair, he sat up and cast a furious glance at the two unwelcome arrivals. Then he grabbed his pen and prepared to make an entry in the ledger. After filling in all data relating to the prisoner, such as age, profession, and marital status, he stopped and asked:

"Why did you arrest him, officer?"

And with the prompt assurance of a man who really knows what he is talking about, "The Rat" answered:

"For fooling around on the public thoroughfare with *inamible* animals, sir."

The officer of the guard leaned forward, ready to ask Tapia for the meaning of this word, which he now heard for the first time, when a harrying thought restrained him. If the word had been used correctly, his ignorance of it would certainly make him lose face, because once he had corrected this subordinate for a similar error, and later on the man had given him an unpleasant jolt by proving that it was he himself who had been mistaken. He would allow nothing like that to happen again. Besides, it would disrupt the basic tenets of discipline if an inferior proved his superior to be wrong. Moreover, since the word referred to a carriage driver, it no doubt had something to do with horses. They had probably been forced to work under poor conditions, perhaps when sick or injured. This interpretation seemed to satisfy him, and once reassured, he addressed the culprit:

"Is it true? What do you have to say for yourself?"

"Yes, sir; only I didn't know there was a law against it."

This reply, which seemed to confirm the idea that the word had been used correctly, ended the officer's hesitation. As soon as he had finished writing, he gave the policeman his orders:

"Lock him up," he said.

Shortly afterwards, the offender, his captor, and the officer went to see the prefect of police. The latter, who had just received a telephone call from the government, was eager to be off.

"Is the report finished?" he asked.

"Yes, sir," the officer replied.

And thereupon he handed the paper to his superior.

The prefect read it aloud, and when he happened to come upon the unknown word, he paused as if to say:

"What does this mean?" But he did not put his question into words. The fear of seeming ignorant in the eyes of his subordinates sealed his lips. After all, one must look out for the prestige of the hierarchy. Then he breathed a sigh of relief, remembering that the report had been made out by the officer of the guard, who was an expert at his job, and who must have been quite sure it was the right word when he had penned it with such assurance. This made good sense to him, so he decided to postpone consulting the dictionary until he had time to clear the matter up. Now he faced the defendant, asking:

"What do you have to say for yourself? Is it true, what they accuse you of?"

"Yes, your Honor, I don't deny it. But I didn't know there was a law against it."

The prefect shrugged his shoulders, signed the report, and handed it to the officer.

"Take him to court," he ordered.

A substitute judge was presiding at the bench. He was a beardless young man, sent as a temporary replacement for the regular judge, who that day was ill. After reading the report aloud, he addressed the defendant:

"What do you have to say for yourself? Do you deny the accusation?"

The prisoner repeated what he had said before:

"No, your Honor, I don't deny it, but I didn't know there was a law against it."

The magistrate motioned, as if to say:

"Well, I've heard that old song before." Then he lifted his pen and jotted a few lines at the foot of the police report, which he promptly returned to the officer.

"Twenty days or twenty pesos," he said, and all the while he was passing sentence, he glared sternly at the defendant.

When "The Rat" re-entered headquarters, he found the officer of the guard jotting down some notes in the "blotter." He came up to the desk and said:

"The culprit's in jail, sir."

"Did the judge sentence him?"

"Yes, sir to twenty days or a twenty-peso fine. And he can't pay the fine because one of his buggy-springs is broken and he hasn't been able to drive around for several days."

The officer was flabbergasted.

"But if he wasn't driving, how could he have violated any traffic laws?"

"It had nothing to wo with traffic laws, sir."

"How else can it be, then? Didn't you mention something about animals?"

"Yes, sir, I did, but they were *inamible* animals. And as you know, there are only three kinds of *inamible* animals: toads, snakes, and lizards. Martin caught a snake on the hill and went around the street with it, frightening people. It was my duty to arrest him, and I did."

The officer was so amazed that he stammered: "*Inamible?* What makes them *inamible?*"

The sly, petulant face of "The Rat" expressed the greatest wonder. Whenever he coined a word, it never occurred to him that he had originated it. He honestly believed it had always been in the language, and that if others did not know it, it was out of sheer ignorance. This was the reason for the supercilious way in which he replied:

"Toads, snakes, and lizards frighten people who see them suddenly and leave them *inamible*, that is, without a drop of *animus*, or courage. Therefore, they are referred to as *inamible*, sir."

When alone again, the officer collapsed in his chair and lifted his arms in desperation. He was terrified. He had put his foot in it, accepting the cursed word without further investigation. And all at once he was dismayed to find that his error had set in motion a fateful chain of events. Good heavens! What a hullaballoo if this mess came to light! What if it had already! He ought to have spoken up, and told the court that the word was not listed in any dictionary.

But that was nothing. What if the publisher of "The Dart," who was constantly attacking public officials, got wind of it! What a scandal! He could already hear the whole town laughing at the expense of the police authorities.

He rose from his seat and paced nervously about the room, intent on finding some means of rectifying an error for which he considered himself alone responsible.

All at once he went up to the desk, dipped his pen in

the inkwell, lifted it over the last annotation on the open pages of the "blotter," aimed, and let go, scoring a direct hit on the word which had caused him so much trouble. For a moment he eyed his work critically, then regarded it with apparent satisfaction. The accursed word was now illegible and hidden safely under an enormous blot. But this was not enough; he must do the same to the police report. Luckily for him, his cousin was a clerk in the jailer's office and would be alone today because the jailer had been taken ill. He lost no time getting to the jailhouse, which was only a stone's throw from headquarters, and as he entered, the first thing he saw was the report, lying on the desk under a paperweight. Taking advantage of his cousin's momentary absence, he sought out the word he had so carelessly put into circulation and drowned it under an inkblot. Now he breathed a sigh of relief. The danger had been averted, and there could be no repercussions.

On his way back from the jailhouse, he suddenly remembered the carriage driver, and a shadow of displeasure crossed his face. Now he paused, and mumbled under his breath:

"I know what I've got to do," he said. "Then everything will be all fixed up."

Meanwhile, the prefect had not been able to forget the strange word he had let pass on a document bearing his signature. He had let it go by without questioning because other, more urgent matters had required his immediate attention. But afterwards he became vaguely frightened, and his fear increased considerably when he found out that the suspicious word was not in the dictionary.

Without losing any time, he started toward the officer of the guard's office, determined to thrash out the matter once and for all. But when he reached the door at the end of the corridor, he saw "The Rat," who had just come from the jailhouse to report on the completion of the errand with which he had been entrusted. The prefect now eavesdropped on their conversation, not missing a single syllable, and what he heard left him so astounded and angry that he could not stir from the spot.

When the policeman had gone out, he entered and walked up to the desk to examine the "blotter." The inksplotch, which had obliterated the hateful word, also had the strange effect of calming his nerves.

Then all at once he realized that at this very moment his subordinate was probably at the jailhouse repeating the same operation on the accursed paper he had so unwisely signed.

And since it was practically a matter of life or death, he planned to make a personal check-up to make sure the face-saving blot had kept the sword of Damocles from falling on his head.

On leaving the jailer's office, the prefect smiled serenely. Now there was nothing to fear; his streak of bad luck was at an end. But as he crossed the vestibule, he happened to see a group of convicts behind bars, and his face took on a worried look. This mess is still at loose ends, he thought. Yet perhaps a solution was not too far off.

"That's what has to be done," he whispered to himself, "then everything will be all right."

That day the judge had left court a bit earlier than usual, and on arriving home, was surprised to find "The Rat" standing at attention at the front door. The latter had been assigned to the first shift of a permanent post at the magistrate's house, and seeing him made the judge recall the peculiar word on the police report which was for him still an enigma. It was not listed in the dictionary, and no matter how much he searched his memory, he could find no trace of any word even remotely like it.

Since he was burning up with curiosity, he decided to question the policeman diplomatically and thus worm

some information out of him. He answered Tapia's salute
and smiled pleasantly as he spoke:

"I congratulate you for your zeal in pursuing those
who mistreat animals," he said. "There are many cruel
people like that carriage driver you arrested this morning
for maltreating tired and wounded horses."

As the magistrate uttered these words, "The Rat's"
face changed expression. The humble smile and respectful look disappeared and were replaced by an imperti-
nent, contemptuous smirk. Then, with an emphatically
ironic air of bravado, he made a precise report of the
facts, repeating what he had told the officer of the guard
at headquarters.

Although he managed to keep a straight face, the
judge was so tickled by the story that he burst out laughing the moment he entered the house. Suddenly the memory of the carriage driver whom he had sent to jail for
an imaginary crime brought his gaiety to a stop. Seated
at his desk, he thought the matter over for a long while,
and then, as if he had found the solution to a very difficult problem, he said in a very low voice:

"Yes, there's no doubt about it, it's the best, most
practical solution..."

On the morning following his arrest, the carriage
driver was brought before the jailer, who handed him
three typewritten envelopes addressed as follows:

"Mr. Martin Escobar, c/o the XXX Jail."

Inside each of them was a twenty-peso bill. No written matter accompanied the mysterious remittances. The
jailer gave the prisoner the money and told him smilingly:

"Take it, friend, this is yours, it belongs to you."

The culprit took two bills and left the third on the
table, saying:

"That's to pay the fine, jailer."

A moment later, the carriage driver was in the
street, feasting his eyes lovingly on the two bills.

"As soon as it's all spent," he remarked, "I'll go up the hill, catch one of those *inamible* animals, find 'The Rat,' and the next day, paf! I'll put three pieces of paper like this in my pocket."

THE TRAP

On a cold, foggy morning in June, two friends sat chatting merrily over breakfast in the large old dining room of the ranch, "El Laurel." Luis Rivera. who leased and ran the ranch, and Antonio del Solar, a lieutenant in the Engineering Corps, were young men, about twenty-five or twenty-six, who had been good friends since their school days together. Del Solar, whose regiment was garrisoned in a nearby village, made frequent visits to the ranch because he was extremely fond of hunting. He had arrived, the afternoon before, much to the lonely Rivera's joy, to spend a couple of days indulging in his favorite sport.

Just when the two friends were most enthusiastically engrossed in conversation, rapid hoofbeats resounded in the patio and then the clanking noise of spurs approached the dining room door. In the threshold appeared Joaquín, the old major-domo. A thick poncho hung from his shoulders and enormous leather chaps covered his legs way up over his knees. Hat in hand, he advanced a few steps and stopped respectfully before the two young men.

"What's the matter, Joaquín? Have you something to tell me?"

As the old man answered, his voice trembled slightly:

"Yes, sir. I bring bad news. Last night they skinned another one of our animals in 'Los Sauces' pasture."

Rivera's face reddened, but since he said nothing,

the old man added: "It was the spotted cow, sir, the one we call 'La Manchada.' "

Rivera's fist banged the table and he jumped to his feet exclaiming angrily:

"What! 'La Manchada'! —and why was she in 'Los Sauces'? Who put her there?"

"They took her out of the little pasture, sir, and put her there to kill her."

Rivera sank back on his chair, looked at his friend and then to explain his outburst, said, "She was a fine cow, Antonio. I bought her at the fair just a short while ago for a thousand pesos."

Turning to Joaquín, Rivera asked:

"How did they get her out of the little pasture?"

"They slipped the bars in the fence in the corner next to 'Los Sauces.' "

"And didn't Agustín hear anything? Didn't the dogs bark?"

"He says not, sir."

"Well, you know what has to be done. You may go." But just as the old man crossed the doorstep, another question stopped him:

"What did they take?"

"The skin, sir, the tongue and a hunk of loin."

"Always the same old things," said Rivera to his friend. Then he added: "These losses are really discouraging me, Antonio. Believe me, sometimes I've thought of giving the whole thing up, cancelling my lease and leaving this cursed land with its plague of cattle thieves. Last year they got eight of my animals and last night's loss makes four in the last five months."

Del Solar had been silent. Now he fixed his serene, penetrating blue eyes on his friend's sunburned, energetic face.

"And you, what have you done to stop this plague?"

"All that I could. I organized the night watches in the pastures. I even take part in them most of the time.

I offered a two-hundred-peso reward. For two weeks, I had a secret agent here disguised as a cowhand. Result— nothing. No matter how much I rack my brain, I haven't been able to discover a way of catching the thieves."

"And the police, what have they done?"

"Well, I'll tell you. At first, whenever they killed an animal, I rode straight to the village to complain to the police. I not only spoke to the chief, I even went to the judge and the governor. They all kept assuring that very soon the culprits would be brought to justice. With these promises, I'd come back to the ranch sure that soon they'd be captured. But as time went by, and in spite of all our vigilance the thieves just kept right on, I lost all confidence in the police. Now, I merely write them a letter letting them know what has happened and describing the color and markings of the dead animal."

"Well, that takes care of the police. But, what about all the other ranchers around here? They must have suffered. They wouldn't have picked you out as the only victim."

"Of course not, they have had the same trouble. Vargas, Fernández and Sandoval, the nearest ones, have been harder hit than I. Not a week goes by that they don't get one or two of their herd."

"What do they do about it?"

"We've had several meetings about it. But every- thing we do fails. These scoundrels are so clever, that we are beginning to wonder whether anyone will ever be able to catch them."

Del Solar agreed, "They must be pretty clever. How do they operate?"

"It's very simple. They go into a pasture, tie the animal to a tree or a fence post. Immediately, with a sharp pointed knife, they strike at the back of the neck into the spinal cord. Quick as a flash, the victim falls flat. They tear off the skin, cut a piece of choice meat and escape with the spoils."

The lieutenant protested vigorously:

"What barbarians! That means they must skin them alive because cutting the cord would stun but not kill the animal immediately."

"That's right, Antonio, and besides, as they don't stop to quarter and bleed the animal, the meat isn't much good and has to be sold for almost nothing. They must get about twenty or thirty pesos for the hide and, for that miserable sum, they waste twenty or thirty times that much, so it is no good to anyone. If they took the whole live animal, it wouldn't seem so bad."

"I agree, Luis. This way it is twice as bad. But, do they use any light? A lantern or something? How do they see?"

"No, they use no light. They work by touch. The light from a match or a cigarette would give them away."

"Then the thief must be a butcher by profession because the place where the knife has to hit is between the first and second vertebrae just back of the horns. In the slaughterhouse, I've seen them do it lots of times and it surprises me that anyone could do it in the dark. Either this fellow has cat's eyes or he's an expert."

The rancher spoke up: "No matter how dark the night, it is always possible to see a short distance. Besides, these men are used to working in the dark. There can be no doubt that this one has a very practiced hand, because a slip of only one or two centimetres would mean failure, as the animal would go wild and set up such a bellowing that the whole ranch would know it."

"Since they work in absolute silence, they would immediately run, wouldn't they?"

"That's what they would do. No doubt about it."

"There's another thing that occurrs to me, Luis. Those devils must have spies inside the ranches. Someone must tell them where the animals are, the nights when there are no watches, etc."

"I think so, too, Antonio. I've fired everybody that I had any suspicion about. So have my neighbors. Actually, I have only one man now that I suspect, but we are keeping a close watch on him and at the slightest proof I'll throw him out as I did the others."

"These precautionary methods seem fine, Luis, but these thieves are so crafty and wary that it isn't going to be easy to catch them redhanded."

"Oh, it's true that they are clever, but I've had years of experience with men of this type and they don't fool me. They are primitive souls that any man with half an eye can figure out."

Del Solar smiled. "Just a minute, now," he said, "that can't be such good insight, nor these primitive souls so simple if you and your friends are being run ragged! I'm sure they must know their business down to the smallest detail!"

Rivera had to smile too. "You're right. When it comes to stealing, these rustics display a superior intelligence. Not even the devil would think up some of the tricks that they use to rob and hide their crimes."

The two friends continued their discussion for another fifteen minutes. Del Solar seemed intensely interested in the subject. He took in every word Rivera said. Finally, he stood up.

"I have an idea," he said, "but I need time to think it over. When I have it all worked out, I'll let you know. Right now I'm going to take a few potshots at those wild pigeons out in the pasture."

"Go right ahead. You'll find lots of them out at 'Los Sauces.' Flocks of them gather there every morning. Sorry I can't come with you but I have to go over some accounts and write my little letter of complaint to the chief of police!"

At noon the host and his guest met again in the dining room. As they lunched, del Solar regaled his friend with the accounts of his hunting prowess. But the conversation soon turned again to the cattle thieves. Del Solar told Rivera that he had seen the remains of the cow, had examined the wound very carefully and that he was sure his idea could be carried out. But it had one drawback. It would be costly. Another animal would have to be sacrificed.

"I'd sacrifice not only one, but two or three, to get my hands on that gang," exclaimed Rivera, eyes flashing and his whole face lit up with anger.

"Then, it's a deal," declared del Solar. "But it will have to be a secret. There are certain details that will have to be gone over very carefully. This afternoon, I'll go back to the village and when everything is ready, I'll let you know. I suppose last night's foray won't be repeated right away and that it will be some time before the next raid?"

"Well, perhaps," was the rancher's doubtful reply, "but you can't be too sure. Last year they killed two of my cows in one week."

A week later, Lieutenant del Solar galloped into the patio of " El Laurel" and dismounted. He met Rivera on the wide veranda, then they both went to a small room that served as an office. An hour later, the two galloped away across the pastures, followed closely by Joaquín.

It was ten o'clock in the morning and the soft rays of a pale sun lit up the beautiful panorama of fertile fields. "El Laurel" was made up of low grazing lands and gently rolling hills that were subdivided by miles of crossbar wooden fences, the kind of enclosure that is used in southern Chile, not like the stone or adobe walls used in the central and northern regions.

After a ten-minute ride, the three horsemen entered a large pasture where oxen and cows were nibbling at the lush green grass still glistening with morning dew. Rivera pointed:

"Those are work oxen, Antonio. You can choose the one you want."

Del Solar rode nearer and examined them carefully. Then, pointing out a handsome roan whose uplifted horns showed his native origin, he declared, "This one will do. Is he tame?"

Joaquín hastened to reply, "As tame as anything, sir. 'El Cordillera' is tame as a lamb."

"Drive him toward 'Los Pidenes' corral."

"Los Pidenes" was an enclosure about a quarter of a mile long, shut in by thick crossbars of heavy wood. No sooner were they all inside than the soldier and the major-domo dismounted and approached the ox.

"Get a little closer, sir," said Joaquín. "See how tame he is?" And the rough old hand stroked the head of the gentle beast who made no move to get away. The lieutenant buried his hand in the thick hair of the animal's neck and asked the old man:

"Is this where the knife should strike, Joaquín?"

"Yes, sir, one stab there near the horns and they fall like a load of lead."

From the pocket of his jacket del Solar extracted a cylindrical object that looked like the piece of an untanned leather strap about sixty centimetres long. He placed it like a bow knot around the bottom of the horns and then tied it together with little wires that protruded from either end. Next he drew from his pocket a roll of red wire and fastened it securely so it would stay in place. Then, stepping back, he contemplated his work with complete satisfaction and said to Rivera, who had quietly taken in the whole operation:

"Just right, Luis. Not one centimetre out of the way. Look how it falls in just the right place. If our friend doesn't want to miss his target, he'll have to remove the obstacle." Turning for the major-domo's opinion, he asked, "What do you say, Joaquín? When they find something in the way, what will they do? Will they untie it or what do you think?"

"As they're in such a hurry, sir, they'll not waste time untying it. They'll cut it with a knife."

"That's what I think, too," affirmed the lieutenant. Then after a pause, he added: "But don't you think they'll wonder, get suspicious?"

The major-domo reassured him, "No, sir. They'll think it is some identification strap that has been put on the animal."

On the way back, Rivera issued his final instructions to Joaquín: "You are to tell everyone that 'El Cordillera' has hoof and mouth disease and that he has been isolated in the corral to keep the other animals from catching it. You will also watch out that no one get anywhere near him."

The old man bowed respectfully. "Everything will be done as you say, sir."

Late that afternoon, with his game bag full of pigeons, del Solar said goodbye to his friend with these words:

"The trap is set. Now all we have to do is sit back and wait."

* * *

Some time later, one Sunday morning, in the officers' club, del Solar read aloud to his companions a letter he had just received from his friend Rivera. It bore the postmark of the town which the battalion of engineers had left. The unit had been transferred to a garrison further north. The rancher of "El Laurel" wrote:

My dear Antonio:

The trap worked beautifully and, thanks to it, the whole gang of thieves is now in jail. So that you may know how successful your ingenious invention was, I'll give you a brief account of what happened.

As we had agreed, I tightened up the night watch. On the fifth day of this, with the pretext that other places needed it more, I ordered the watch on "Los Pidenes" to be held only every other night. The spy in our midst—and I was right; it was the one I told you about—must have given the news to his accomplices, because last Thursday, when there was no watch, they decided to strike. That night I went to bed early. The continuous watches had me worn out and I slept like a log until two in the morning. Then I got up, dressed quickly and joined Joaquín, who had the horses ready in the patio.

No sooner did we get to the corral than we made out the shadow of the fallen ox on the ground next to the fence. We dismounted, lit the lantern we had brought and after we had looked at the motionless ox, with its head all blown off, we began to look for tracks around it. Right on the edge near the fence we found bloodstains on the grass. We followed the traces for a long time until we reached the main road. There the hoofprints of several horses told us that the wounded man and his friends must be far away. We retraced our steps and renewed the search around poor dead "Cordillera." Almost immediately, we tripped over a sack which contained coils of rope and various butcher knives. We had just finished looking these over when I heard Joaquín shout:

"Sir! Come see what's here!"

I took a few steps and by the light of the lantern saw, lying there on the grass, a hand that had been severed above the wrist. It was still bleeding. Although I'm not a bit timid, the sight of it gave me the shivers. That enormous muscular hand still held in its rigid fingers the handle of a wide, sharp-bladed knife.

From the enclosed clipping you can read all the details of how the police caught the culprit. As you guessed, he is an old slaughterhouse employee who preferred this kind of night work, considering it to be more lucrative, no doubt. As he has completely confessed his crimes and denounced all his accomplices, the whole gang has been incarcerated. Now we can go on with our work without all the fears and worries to which we have been victim for so long.

When del Solar had finished the letter a voice was heard to ask: "And the trap, how did you make the trap?"

"It was really very simple. It was a hard rubber tube, filled with two hundred grams of dynamite. So that it would look completely harmless, it was lined with rabbit skin. There were two detonators in it attached to the wires that came out both ends. Any light pressure on any part of this ring, placed around the base of the horns, would produce an explosion."

"Very ingenious," said the same voice, "but it seems to me a bit brutal."

Del Solar replied heatedly: "Anyone can see, Enrique, that you don't know anything at all about the cattle thieving that is the shameful and ugly plague that infests our land. If you knew it as I do, you would change your mind."

Enrique was about to reply, but just then the arrival of two new officers put an end to the argument.

SUB-SOLE

Seated on the sifted sand, while her baby avidly assuaged its hunger at her firm round breast, Cipriana, her eyes shining and moist from the stimulating exercise of her walk, gazed out upon the liquid plain of the sea.

For some minutes she forgot her difficult trek over the sands as she contemplated the magic panorama that unfolded before her eyes. The water, in which was reflected the celestial arch of the sky, was a deep blue. The tranquility of the air and the calmness of the low tide gave the ocean the appearance of a diaphanous, still pond. Not a single wave rippled its smooth, glassy surface. Way off in the distance, on the line of the horizon, the sail of a ship in no way disturbed the august solitude of the quiet waters.

After a brief rest, Cipriana stood up. She still had a long way to go to reach her destination. On her right, a high promontory that reached out into the sea revealed its steep, bare cliffs, devoid of all vegetation and, on her left, the long beach of fine, white sand stretched toward the dark string of hills that rose in the east. The young woman swung a straw basket from her right hand and she carried, snuggled against her, the sleeping child wrapped in the folds of her wool shawl. Its brilliant scarlet and green colors contrasted sharply with the monotonous gray of the sand dunes. She slowly descended the sandy dune and began to walk along the beach. The outgoing tide had left uncovered a wide strip of slightly moist sand on which the woman's feet left but a light footprint. Not a single human being was in sight for as far as the eye could see. While a few gulls frolicked in the white ribbons of foam, enormous pelicans, with their open wings poised, glided one after the other, like comets suspended on a single invisible string, over the sleepy waters. Their fantastic silhouettes lengthened out into enormous shadows on the dunes, then suddenly, rounding the promontory, they were lost to view on the deep ocean.

After half an hour's walk, Cipriana was confronted with great blocks of stone that cut off her path. Here the shore grew narrow and then disappeared beneath great slabs of deeply crevassed basalt rock. She jumped lightly over the obstacles, turning left, and suddenly she was in a little open cove between the high walls of a deep crevice.

Here the beach appeared again, short and narrow. The pale, gold sand stretched like a very fine carpet round the dark semicircle that girded in the little inlet.

The mother's first care was to locate a spot where she might shelter her baby from the hot rays of the sun. This she soon found in the shade of a large cliff whose sides, still wet, bore the indelible mark of the onslaught of the waves.

When she had chosen the driest spot, furthest from the water's edge, she unwound from her shoulders her long, spacious shawl and with it made a soft bed for the sleeping child. With loving care so as not to awaken him, she laid him into that improvised nest.

He was very well developed for a ten-month-old baby, white and plump, with large eyes now hidden by delicate, transparent, pink lids.

For some minutes the mother stood ecstatically drinking in that beautiful, sweet face. She herself was dark, of average height, with black, thick hair and not at all beautiful. Her commonplace features lacked refinement and were unattractive. She had a large mouth, with thick lips, the strong white teeth of a country girl; her small brown eyes were somewhat humble and without expression.

But when she turned to the baby, the lines of her face softened, the eyes lit up with a brilliance of passionate intensity and her whole ugly visage became soft and beautiful.

The sun, high above the horizon now, flooded with light the little spot of incomparable beauty. The sides of the cliff disappeared beneath the tangled web of bushes and climbing vines. Above the light hum of the insects and the soft murmur of the waves against the rocks, from the thicket rose at intervals the melancholy cry of the *pitio*. The calmness of the ocean, the stillness of the air and the tranquility of the heavens had in them something of the sweetness that was reflected on the child's face and that shone in the mother's eyes. In spite of herself, Cipriana was caught in the spell of the irresistible magic of the beauty all about her.

Turning toward the water's edge, she examined the little beach, in front of which there extended for about fifty meters into the sea a vast rock shelf. The surface was smooth and shiny, broken by innumerable crevices that were covered over with sea moss and different species of marine plants.

Cipriana took off her heavy shoes, tucked up about her waist her faded percale skirt, and picking up her basket, crossed the dry beach and advanced onto the slippery wet stones. She bent over to examine every crevice that she came across. All kinds of shellfish lined these holes. With the help of a small iron hook, Cipriana dislodged them from the rock and threw them into her basket. From time to time she interrupted her task to cast a quick glance at the baby who still slept quietly on.

The ocean resembled a vast, turquoise blue lagoon. Although the hour of ebb tide had already gone, the influx rose with such slowness that only an experienced eye would have noticed that the visible part of the rock was diminishing imperceptibly. The water was washing in with increasing force and greater volume along the rock openings.

Cipriana went on with her task without hurrying. She knew the place well and at this hour she had plenty of time before she would have to abandon the rocky shelf as it disappeared beneath the waves.

The basket was rapidly filling. Between the transparent leaves of the sea lettuce, the gray tones of the snails and the silvery gleam of the schools of minnows stood out. Cipriana, her body bent over, the basket in one hand and the hook in the other, went to and fro surefootedly on that slippery surface. Her tight waist revealed the base of her round, dark neck. Her eyes quickly scrutinized the cracks. Every time she found a shellfish, she yanked it from the sharp surface of the rock. From time to time she straightened up to fasten back the heavy black braids. The vigorous lines of the large awkward peasant body with its wide hips were not lacking in grace and beauty. The warm kiss of the sun brightened her fat cheeks and the fresh air with which she filled her lungs made the young blood boil in the veins of this robust girl in the springtime of her life.

Time went on. The tide was slowly rising, invading little by little the lower parts of the rock slab. Suddenly, Cipriana stopped and looked searchingly into one of the crevices. Then she stood up, took a step away; but almost immediately she turned back again and stopped once more in the same place. What caught her attention and made her turn back was the shell of a snail that lay there at the bottom of a small opening. Although tiny, of a very rare and strange shape, it appeared magnified when seen through the crystalline water.

Cipriana knelt and thrust her right hand into the opening, but to no avail, for the crack was too narrow and she could scarcely touch this mother-of-pearl object with her fingertips. But the slight contact only quickened her desire. She withdrew her hand, vacillated for a second, but the thought that it would make a beautiful plaything for her baby, that would cost nothing, urged her on.

The rose-pink tone of the shell with its changing, iridescent lights stood out so softly against its green, velvety background. Making a new attempt, she overcame the difficulty and picked up the precious shell. But when she went to withdraw her hand, she could not. In vain did she struggle to free herself. Every effort proved useless. She was caught in a trap. The shape of the crack and the slippery sides had made it possible that she slide her hand with great difficulty through the narrow mouth which, now circling her wrist like a tight bracelet, held in its grip her work-hardened hand.

At first, Cipriana felt only a slight annoyance but that gradually transformed itself into a frustrated rage, as all her efforts became more and more futile. Then a vague anguish, a growing anxiety began to overpower her spirit. Her heartbeat quickened and a cold perspiration bathed her brows. Suddenly her blood froze within her, her eyes opened wide and a nervous trembling shook her from head to foot. Her eyes and face distorted with fear, she saw before her a white, moving line that advanced a little way on the beach and then withdrew rapidly. It was the foam of a wave. She beheld graphically and clearly in her imagination the horrible vision of her son dragged and tossed in the flow of the tide. She uttered a penetrating howl that echoed back from the cliffs, slid over the waters and then faded away onto the watery vastnesses of the sea.

Kneeling on the rock, she struggled furiously for a few minutes. Under the tension of her muscles, her joints cracked and were dislocated. Her shrieks threw panic into the winged populace that fed here near the inlet:

gulls, crows, sea swallows, all rose in terrified flight and quickly disappeared beneath the radiant splendor of the sun.

Cipriana looked dreadful. Her perspiration-soaked clothes stuck to her skin. Her unbraided hair half covered her atrociously disfigured face; her cheeks were sunken in and her eyes blazed. She had stopped shrieking and her eyes were fixed on the small bundle that lay on the beach as she tried to calculate how long it would be before the waves reached it. It would not be long because the tide was already rising with greater speed and very soon only a few centimeters of the rock shelf remained above the water.

The ocean, which had been so tranquil until then, began to swell and spasmodic upheavals began to shiver across its shining surface. Light curlings, small ripples disturbed its blue, smooth calmness. With a caressing and rhythmical swish, the soft waves beat against the sides of the rock and deposited on the sand white plumes of foam, that beneath the burning rays of the sun took on changing tones of mother-of-pearl or rainbow hues. The hidden cove was permeated with an atmosphere of perfect peace. Through the soft, quiet air, laden with the salty tang of the ocean, wafted the sounds of the waves lapping against the rocks, the insects and the far away cry of the sea gulls.

Cipriana, completely exhausted by her terrible struggles to free herself, looked imploringly about her but saw neither on land nor sea a single living human being who might help her. In vain, she cried out to her family, to the mother that had borne her, to her husband, the father of her child, who there behind the dunes in their poor humble home awaited her return. Not a voice answered. Then she turned her gaze on high and the love for her child tore from her unversed, anguished and tortured soul words and pleas of heart-rending eloquence:

"Dear God, have pity on my son, save him, help him.

Pardon for my little son, oh Lord. Holy Virgin, defend him. Take my life, not his. Holy mother, let me take out my hand so I may move him to safety. One moment, just one little moment... I swear, I'll come back again. I'll let the water swallow me up, let my body be broken to pieces on these rocks. I'll not move and I'll die blessing you. Holy Virgin, keep back the waters, stop the waves. Don't let me die in desperation... Mercy, oh Lord. Pity, Heavenly Father. Hear me, oh most Holy Virgin. Listen to me, Dear Mother!"

But above, the heavens, without a shadow, without a sign, diaphanous and unfathomable as infinite space, gave back no reply.

The first wave that hit the rock shelf tore from the mother one last cry of mad desperation. Then from her throat there rose only the hoarse, muted gurglings that sounded like the rattle of the dying.

The coldness of the water revived Cipriana's failing strength. The struggle to slip her hand from the crack began again more furiously and agonizingly than before. The violent pulling and the rubbing of her flesh against the rock had made her arm swell, so the granite ring that held it only tightened about her wrist.

The liquid mass, rising constantly, finally covered the rock. Only the head and shoulders of the kneeling woman remained above the surface. From then on, the tide rose so rapidly that soon the waves reached the place where the baby lay. A few more minutes, then the inevitable happened. A long wave licked at the sleeping child. When it felt the cold of that harsh bath, the child awoke, squirmed like a worm, then uttered a penetrating, shrill cry.

That her martyrdom might be complete, Cipriana was not spared even the slightest detail of this scene. When she heard the cry, that tore at the very depths of her being, a wave of madness swept over her. Just as an animal caught in a trap bites off the imprisoned limb, so Cipriana, her hungry mouth ready, bent toward the rock. But even this last recourse was denied her. The water that now reached her neck forced her to keep her head high.

On the beach, the waves came and went happily, playfully tossing and turning the little boy. They stripped off his swaddling clothes. All that was left was his little white shirt and his small, plump body rolled in the foam as he desperately wriggled his tiny arms and legs. The shock of the water and the brusque, endless rubbing over the sand made his firm delicate skin, touched by the sun's rays, shine and glisten.

Cipriana, her neck stretched, her eyes bulging, as she gazed at that scene, was suddenly shaken by a violent convulsion. In the paroxysm of her grief, her reason gave way. Her vision dimmed. The light of her spirit was swept away and as her energy and vigor succumbed, her body, too, slumped. Her head sank into the water. A little whirlpool stirred the waters and some bubbles apeared on the tranquil surface of the full tide.

The baby, plaything of the waves, cried less and less frequently. The ocean, like a loving nurse, tried to quiet him, redoubled its caresses, sang it sweetest songs, solicitously and tirelessly turned him over and over and rocked him from side to side.

At last his crying ceased. He had gone to sleep. Although his little face was livid, his eyes and mouth full of sand, his sleep was peaceful; but so profound that when the tide dragged him into the sea and deposited him on the bottom, he woke no more.

And while heaven stretched its blue canopy over all land and sea, where life and death are perpetually intertwined, the infinite grief of this mother, which if divided among all the souls of the earth was great enough to silence all men, failed to cast even the slightest shadow on the divine harmony of that palpitating scene of life, sweetness, peace and love.

IN THE TENEMENT HOUSE

Between two rows of squalid habitations, whose sordidness bore witness to the landlord's negligence and avarice, extended a patio about fifteen metres wide and forty long, strung with wires and rope from which hung clothes of all sizes and colors.

The dwellings, separated by thin partitions, had no windows and but one door, in the upper part of which were a few holes that provided the only ventilation.

Workmen and laborers lived here. The janitress lived in the largest quarters facing the street and her job entailed the important functions of collecting the rents and ejecting all those who were either remiss in their payments or lacking in the respect and deference due such a high and mighty representative of the landlord.

One cold, cloudy, winter morning, the ragged women and children were gathered in the doorways. Outside, in the patio, some washerwomen, their bare arms blue with cold, bent over their tubs, scrubbing clothes in soapy water.

Suddenly, from one of the rooms ran screaming a little six or seven-year-old girl, closely followed by a woman who shrieked angrily after her:

"Stop! I tell you to stop!"

But the lively little girl agilely slipped between the tubs, barrels and all the other things that littered the patio. Convinced that pursuit was useless, the woman went back to her room, but not before she had threatened the runaway:

"A spanking's nothing to what you'll get when I catch up with you, you little rascal!"

But the mischievous child just twisted up her little dark features and made funny faces to show you could not scare her with any old threats.

The room to which the woman returned was cluttered with junk. A table, covered with an old oilcloth, occupied the center of the room. Two iron cots stood against the wall. Scattered over the floor were buckets of lye, bundles of clothes, pots and pans of all kinds. Near the door, in a large divided cage, were several gamecocks.

As soon as she entered, the woman —her name was Sabina— resumed the ironing she had interrupted to punish that little devil, Berta, who nearly drove her crazy with her naughty tricks. Loud, infuriated shrieks behind her obliged her to turn and shout angrily:

"Aida, what *are* you doing to that child?"

"Nothing, Mommie. She's the one. She wont't eat!"

The two girls were sitting on a sack. The older, a nine-year-old with small, lively gray eyes and a round, dark face, was feeding the younger with spoonfuls of milk from a cup that was placed on a box at her right. But, for no apparent cause, from time to time the little girl pushed away the food, waved her arms and shrieked angrily and impatiently. Each time that this occurred, the mother repeated:

"The milk must be too hot. Cool it a little."

Aida followed these instructions to the letter. She blew on the cup and then on the spoon, and before feeding her sister, she tried it herself. Now, this was the detail that escaped the mother and the real reason for the child's fits of temper. As a result of the whole maneuver, the spoon, which always came out of the cup full, reached her hungry mouth half-empty, sometimes with but a few drops.

This fraud, which provoked her desperate outcries, she could neither avoid nor denounce because, although she was three, she could only utter a stammering word or two. Rickets had taken an atrocious toll on the weak little body. She could move only by dragging herself along the floor and all her mother's efforts to make her walk were futile. In her ignorance, Sabina attributed this physical weakness to deliberate obstinacy on the part of the child. That is why, when anyone asked:

"What! Anita not walking yet?" she invariably answered: "It's just that she doesn't want to."

"Could it be that she is paralyzed?"

"No, indeed. You should see her swing her legs about when she's mad! She's not at all paralyzed then! When she's stopped, her legs go limp. It's just a bad habit she's picked up. I'll have to take it out of her with a good whipping."

These words and the tone in which they were uttered made obvious the rancor she held toward the little girl who, in spite of her age, gave her more trouble than a babe in arms.

Sabina, the washerwoman, was a young woman, twenty-eight at the most, very dark, of medium height, worn out features and sad, brown eyes. She was an indefatigable worker who slaved from sunup to sundown at her tiring tasks. Her husband, a baker by trade, handed over only an insignificant part of his weekly forty-peso salary for his family. Because of this, the mother and her children, three boys and three girls, led a miserable and poverty-stricken existence which all her hard work did little to alleviate.

When Onofre, the husband, was sober, they enjoyed a brief respite. The two pesos which were his daily contribution did a little to assuage their hunger. But these periods of well-being were few and far between.

The day would come when the oldest boy, who went to wait for his father and bring home the daily bread, would return empty-handed. Then he would repeat the fatal words:

"Daddy's drinking again."

From then on, the mother had to redouble her tasks, work night and day on extra laundry, cut down on her own food to satisfy the voracious appetites of all those hungry mouths that constantly besieged her with the unending chant:

"Mommie, I want bread, give me bread, Mommie."

Sabina's ironing was nearly done. The still warm clothes formed a heap on top of the bed, from which suddenly rose a weak baby whimper. Some of the pieces had slipped, touched his face and wakened him. Just then, in the doorway, appeared the silhouette of a man. He looked around the room, then asked:

"Where's Daniel?"

Before Sabina could answer, a thin twelve-year-old boy with a dark, intelligent face slipped hastily into the room:

"Here I am, Daddy," he said, as if afraid.

"Did you feed the cocks?"

"Oh yes, Daddy."

"Water?"

"Water, too."

While he questioned, he examined the birds attentively, feeling their crops to find out whether they had been fed and watered, since once he had caught the boy in a flagrant lie.

This time, he seemed satisfied. While Daniel, casting a sidelong glance at his father, slipped out the door again, the latter, seated next to his cocks, observed their comings and goings with profound interest.

The baker, who was thirty-five, tall and of robust build, was a silent, apathetic man. This characteristic became more pronounced when he was drunk. Only one

thing made him loquacious —his favorite passion, his
gamecocks. Illiterate himself, the problem of his children's education worried him not at all. Just getting them
food and clothing was too great a responsibility and one
which he shirked with alarming frequency.

The children, abandoned to their own devices,
grew like weeds, with nothing to impede the atavistic
impulses of their childish, undisciplined and precocious
souls. The older ones lived in the streets and came home
only to sleep. Their love for the father had been killed by
his indifference and the cruel beatings he inflicted, which
were out of all proportion to the crimes committed. Fear
was the dominant sentiment in his presence, which they
fled whenever they could.

As for the mother, she was always too busy to
pay them much attention. Besides, her uneducated mind,
full of superstitions and absurd prejudices, made her a
bad teacher. Unlike her husband, she met her children's
misdoings with shrieks and threats she never carried
out, so she soon lost what little authority she had ever
had. Sure of their impunity, they answered her scoldings
with jeers and even insults.

For some moments, the room was absolutely quiet.
The baby had gone back to sleep and the little cripple,
Anita, was dragging herself over the paved floor toward
her mother, who with her face flushed continued her
ironing without a minute's rest.

Then, suddenly, in burst Berta, chased by her eight-
year-old brother, Ricardo, with a bunch of nettles in his
hand. When he saw his father, he stopped short, turned
on his heels and ran hastily toward the street.

"Mommie, Ricardo pricked my legs," she sobbed.

Onofre rose and looked out, but the culprit was out
of sight. Sabina left her iron and came closer.

"Why? What did you do to him?" she asked.

"Nothing. We were playing; I was the setting hen

and he pricked my legs so I wouldn't get up from the nest."

"And where on earth did he get that idea?"

"Pablo said that Mrs. Ignacio pricked the breasts of her chickens."

Sabina, in spite of her anger, could not help smiling. "Never mind. When I catch him I'll prick his little bottom with the strap!"

Then, remembering what had happened that morning in the patio, as she bathed the dark, little, bruised legs with a vinegar-soaked rag, she whispered:

"That's what you get for being naughty. See how God punishes you for being disobedient?"

But Berta, relieved now of the smart of the prickly spines, was not listening, so anxious was she to join the noisy throng that filled the patio with their shouts. No sooner had her mother finished than off she went again.

Sabina interrupted the subsequent silence:

"Onofre," she said, "Ricardo is going around barefoot and Daniel will soon be doing the same. I'm in debt at the store. They can't go to school without shoes because they won't admit them. If you don't buy them..."

The curt, ironic voice of her husband cut her off:

"You think I'm made of money?"

"No, but you earn enough and give me too little."

"I give you too much."

"You spend more on your own pleasures. Last week you lost fifty pesos on the cockfight."

"That's a lie. I didn't lose a cent because I won it all back."

"You've been telling me that for years," answered his wife, not believing a word of it. "But you never see the money you put on the cockfights again."

"So what? Can't I spend my own money or throw it away as I please?"

"Oh, of course, since your wife and children mean nothing to you."

"Look, you can talk all you want, but a lot of men give their wives less than I do, and nobody makes a fuss about that."

"Because they expect their wives to slave around the house all day and not say a word. When it comes to home it hurts them to even spend a penny, but to go carousing, they throw away their money at the drop of a hat."

Onofre's face turned dark with anger, and instead of answering, he walked to the door and slammed it shut behind him.

Sabina watched him go with a sinking heart. Although experience had shown her how useless it was to complain, she could not resign herself to keeping quiet. For some time, Onofre's lack of cooperation had been making life more and more unbearable. The children ran around barefoot and half-naked and suffered badly from the cold. Since she could lessen these wants only partially, the struggle was becoming increasingly impossible. But she would not admit defeat. With the obstinacy and silent heroism of the women of her class, her valiant spirit never quailed in her unfair fight against misery.

Having finished her ironing, Sabina picked up her baby to nurse him and while the child half-heartedly sucked at her breast, the mother gazed down at the dark, wizened, sickly face. The doctor at the clinic had diagnosed it as an intestinal infection, but all the neighbors and friends, disagreeing, had concluded that the baby had colic. So all the absurd and foolish popular remedies had been tried to cure the affliction. Saturated with ointments and gorged with herb teas, the poor baby agonized for days and weeks, grasping at life with the extraordinary tenacity of his race. Without ever admitting it to herself, deep down, the mother wished that death might extinguish that little wavering light of life that threatened each moment to go out and so free her of one more burdensome anxiety.

She tucked the baby in bed and tidied up the room, stopping to attend to Anita, who had a habit of filling her mouth with the dirt she took from a hole in the wall. She slapped her and pulled her away. At first Anita cried at the top of her lungs, but suddenly, she stopped. She had found a container on the floor with starch and bluing and was daubing the mixture all over her head and face. Sabina shook her again and slapped her even more soundly. Lord, what a child! Always into some mischief.

Going to the door, she called Aida and, pointing to Anita, she ordered, "Take her with you and don't let her eat dirt."

Aida obeyed grudgingly. She showed her resentment by grabbing the child by the arm and shaking her roughly.

Stop it. You and your nasty tricks!" she yelled.

But as she saw her mother bearing down on her menacingly, she fled with the child in her arms, screaming vengefully:

"I'm going to throw her into the ditch —the little devil!"

Since it was nearly noon, Sabina took advantage of these few quiet moments to finish up preparations for lunch. While she diligently scrubbed plates and spoons, the children began to file in and hovered round the pot that bubbled on the coals of the brazier. Their father's absence made them all happy and, declaring a truce to their perpetual quarreling, they laughed and joked merrily without fighting.

Soon the soup was ready and the whole house lapsed into silence. For some moments the only sound to be heard was the clatter of spoons against the plates. Daniel and Ricardo ate standing up, leaning against the table, while Aida and Berta sat on the floor with their legs crossed. At one end of the table, Sabina held Anita in her arms and shared with her the steaming soup, wondering all the while what had happened to Onofre. Could he be out drinking? His absence boded no good. Now she felt almost sorry about upsetting him. Of course, if she had not complained, he might have taken her silence for tacit approval and matters would have been made even worse.

At any rate, she knew he was not bad. He had never mistreated her. His friends were the ones who had dragged him into vice.

The sight of the empty plate which Berta held out to her interrupted Sabina's trend of thought. While she filled it, she marvelled:

"What a child! All of her soup in one swallow!"

Berta was smiling, showing her little, glistening, white teeth and, leaning forward on her small bare toes, she pleaded:

"Meat, too."

"No, I'll divide the meat later."

The rest of them wanted second helpings, too, and when the soup was finished, Sabina divided the meat. She cut it into small pieces, saving the smallest for herself. All of them, except Berta, ate slowly to prolong the pleasure, because meat was such a luxury.

Aida, who was chewing with delight, saw a dirty little hand snatch at the meat on her plate. Before she could stop it, her piece, her precious piece had vanished in a flash. She emitted a desperate yell and threw herself headlong after the thief whom she caught on the threshold. A wild and noisy battle ensued, and it was only with great difficulty that Daniel and Ricardo finally succeeded in separating them. While Aida struggled to free herself and resume the battle, the culprit stood undaunted in the middle of the room with her hands behind her.

When Sabina questioned her about the stolen morsel, licking her lips, with her litttle black eyes sparkling, she answered:

"I swallowed it."

And then, to mitigate the importance of her misdeed, she added:

"It was just a tiny little piece. A weeny bit like this." And she demonstrated with her diminutive thumb and forefinger.

"It was not," contradicted Aida, whimpering. "I had barely tasted it when she grabbed it."

And she would never have stopped crying had not Sabina given up her own piece, to Daniel's great disgust. He saw that his mother had to go without eating all because of those gluttonous girls.

Meanwhile, Anita had fallen asleep on her mother's lap. Sabina contemplated sadly the tiny deformed body and the twisted legs. Gradually a feeling of deep melancholy invaded her spirit and, slowly, one after the other, the tears rolled down her bowed face. It grieved Sabina to see the child so helpless, so defenseless, and to have to admit that perhaps her paralysis was something permanently incurable.

Suddenly, a kind of choked gurgle was heard in the room. Berta and Aida, bursting with laughter, were trying, hands over mouths, to suppress their giggles. Their mother's mute grief, without sobs or moans, seemed to them a funny pantomime which with childish cruelty they tried to imitate, exaggerating the sorrowing gestures with comic seriousness.

Unable to contain themselves, they left the room, driven away by Daniel's furious look. He was not like his sisters. His eyes were wet with tears and his heart heavy. That silent suffering produced in him a painful impression.

Daniel's childish spirit still conserved good qualities which his corrupt and poisonous surroundings had not yet succeeded in destroying. A sharp and quick observer, he already had an experience greater than should be expected of one so young. He was fully aware of the situation created at home by the near desertion of his father. And yet, he did not blame him. In his heart, he secretly admired him. From his earliest childhood, he had reached the conclusion that the law of nature was that man be exempt from all responsibilities. Onofre's squanderings on pleasure —gambling and drinking— meant nothing, since they were a man's prerogatives. He felt proud because he, too, was a man and that one day he would do the same.

Nevertheless, he loved his mother; and seeing her so harassed, he wished he might be older so that he might work for her and help lighten her burden.

The conduct of her first-born was already a great consolation to Sabina. When occasionally a sickness had kept her in bed, Daniel had taken on all her tasks. He had shopped, cooked, taken care of the young ones, and even scrubbed clothes for her like an experienced laundress.

This rough, untrained little boy had a delicate sensitivity that was truly touching when he tried to bring his mother out of her depression. This time, wishing to end her discouragement, he began feverishly to wash the lunch dishes and to straighten the room, walking back and forth in front of her, sneaking little glances in her direction.

This method always worked. His busy coming and going never failed to draw his mother from her melancholy absorption, and as she guessed the child's motives, she grew tender and was comforted by his solicitude.

This time was no exception. Sabina dried her tears and rose to place the sleeping Anita in the drawer which served as her bed. She finished arranging the ironing in a large wicker basket. Daniel, anxious to break the silence, asked:

"Are we going to take the clothes to Miss Luchita's?"

The mother nodded her assent.

"Shall I call Ricardo, then, to help me carry it?"

"No, I'll go myself. I have to collect for the last wash."

Examining the dress she had on, Sabina murmured to herself:

"Heavens! Do I have to go in this?"

"How about the black..." but Daniel did not finish. He suddenly remembered that he, himself, had taken the black dress to the pawnshop some days ago.

Sabina, noting that this had upset and saddened him, said consolingly:

"There's nothing we can do about it, son. If your father would only remember that he has family, we woulnd't have to suffer so much."

Before leaving, the washerwoman charged Ricardo and the two girls with the care of the house, recommending especially that they watch the sick baby and the crippled child. Each one of these instructions was accompanied by a threat: a whipping if they did this, a beating if they didn't do that.

Putting on serious faces, they made believe they understood her warnings and protested they would be good as gold. Sabina, mollified, promised to bring them candies and crackers. This filled them with joy.

No sooner had Daniel and his mother, carrying the basket between them, left the room than they began to discuss what game they would like most to play. After various suggestions, they finally decided to play "store."

The ironing board placed between two boxes served as counted. Behind it knelt Aida, the proprietess, who began immediately to set out her wares: a few handfuls of sand in a tin can. Berta and Ricardo, the customers, made their own money out of little scraps of paper. The transactions were carried out with all the obligatory formality; the buyers bargained, the seller extolled the magnificent quality of her merchandise.

Suddenly, all the chattering stopped. Anita, the cripple, had awakened. Dragging herself noiselessly to the counter, she had taken all the packages that were ready for sale and had torn them open. Aida got up angrily, grabbed her by the arm and hauled her to the furthest corner, paying not the slightest attention to her screams. But a minute later, Anita was back again, a menace to free trade.

Pulling her to the corner again, they placed in her way a barricade of all the chairs and benches in the room. But as Anita overcame all the obstacles their faces were painted with consternation. Aida, however, did not lose courage. She tried a new method. Raising the child in her arms, she carried her over to the hole in the wall, and, pointing, she wheedled:

"Eat some nice little dirt. Here, have some, My, it's good!"

But Anita rejected the attempted bribe, struggling to return to the counter where she too, in her own way, wanted to take part in the game. Her stubbornness so aggravated Aida that she was about to take violent measures when Ricardo proffered:

"Why don't you tie her to the foot of the bed?"

As he looked for a cord or something that would do, his eyes fell on the cocks' cage in which there was an empty compartment.

"Let's put her in here," exclaimed Ricardo.

No sooner said than done. They pushed the screaming Anita into the small space, shut and securely fastened the door.

Crazed with terror at the child's shrieks, the cocks in the neighboring compartments began to crow stridently and beat their wings. Such was the hubbub caused by them on the one hand and the screeching child on the other, that the perpetrators of this little scheme were

terrified at what they had done and tried to undo it.
But when they tried to open the door, they found that
the lock was jammed. Ricardo ran out to the patio to
find a stone to hammer with, but came back immediately, trembling with fear:

"Here comes Daddy," he cried.

He stopped for a moment, not knowing what to do,
then ran out the door as fast as his legs would carry
him. Seconds later, Onofre entered the room. At first,
he stared, paralyzed. But then, seized by a violent rage,
he opened up the cage, took out the little girl and deposited her roughly on the floor. With the cause of the
disturbance eliminated, the cocks began to calm down.
Pale with anger, the baker looked at them: feathers torn
out, crests all bloody, beaks open, panting —they presented a sorry sight.

Onofre, whose fury was increasing with each second, turned to Berta, who, extremely busy behind the
counter, was wrapping and unwrapping packages as
though she knew nothing at all about the tragedy.

"Who put Anita in the cage?" thundered her father.

"Ricardo and Aida did it," was her prompt reply.
"Ricardo ran away and Aida is under the bed."

And to back up her accusation, she went to the cot
and looked under it.

"Here she is, Daddy, way over in the corner."

With an irate voice, stamping on the floor, the
baker ordered the culprit to come out of her hiding place
and he threatened her with a severe punishment. When
she did not obey, he shouted imperiously:

"Berta, bring me a stick!"

Berta ran out and came back immediately, dragging
behind her a long bamboo stick.

"Here it is, Daddy. Poke her with it."

Onofre tried to use it, but the bother of having to
bend way down to the floor made him stop. He dropped
the stick, saying:

"You do it, Berta."

He could not have given her a task more to her liking. She squatted down and, holding on to one end, she directed several furious thrusts under the bed. But a strong tug pulled the stick out of her hand and before she could avoid it, a blow in the chest knocked her violently on her back. Her head hit the stone floor and she uttered a piercing yell.

Onofre, who had been at the cage looking over a cock, came to her asking bad-humoredly:

"What happened? Why are you screaming?"

"It was Aida. She hit me here."

Onofre was furious. He grabbed the stick and was about to lay it on the culprit when a familiar voice called from the doorway. It was an old friend of his, a gamecock dealer, who had come to make him a proposition. Onofre immediately forgot everything to attend to his friend. They held a short conference over by the cage and then they both left, each with a cock under his arm.

As soon as they had gone, Aida emerged from her hiding place and went to her "store." Anita had taken possession of it and had made a shambles of it —the packages were all undone and the sand strewn all over the floor. She hit the child and took away the board.

Ricardo reappeared. First he wanted to know what had happened. Aida told him. Then, with promises and threats, they extracted from Berta a vow of silence so their mother would not find out what had occurred.

Sabina's first thought, when she arrived, was for the baby. He was still sleeping, with that deep, lethargic sleep that had been worrying her for the past few days. After she had asked questions about what had happened in her absence —questions which Ricardo and Aida answered exaggerating the behavior of all— she divided the promised candy and crackers.

As a reward for her discretion, Ricardo and Aida

gave Berta an extra candy and cookie. But no sooner
had she devoured them whole than she turned to her
mother, pointing to the back of her head:

"Mommie, I've a bump back here."

Ricardo and Aida looked daggers at her. But she
went right on complaining until Sabina, feeling the lump,
asked, alarmed:

"How did you do that?"

"Aida knocked me over."

And in spite of the vociferous denials of the culprits
and all their shrieks and threats, she proceeded to re-
late the whole story of Anita and the cage. Sabina, as
usual, yelled and scolded, but they kept out of arms'
reach, looking for a way to avenge Berta's treason.
Right in front of the mother, Ricardo and Aida, one
on the right and the other on the left, closed in on
Berta and they each delivered a mighty punch. They left
her howling and bathed in tears. Sabina ran after them,
but they were so well hidden that she did not even see
them.

The news that Onofre had been there made her feel
better, since it meant that he was no longer angry and
perhaps would come home to sleep.

A little comforted by this hope, she began on the
new washing and worked until sunset. Soon Ricardo
and Aida were back asking for bread. They spoke to
their mother in a tone which was neither respectful nor
humble but rather aggressive and grumbling.

"Mommie, I want bread. Give me some bread,
Mommie."

The laundress, physically and morally exhausted,
finally gave in to their demands, saying:

"Here, you devils. Eat it all up."

When night came, the whole family, with the exception of Onofre, was gathered in the room. After so
much fussing and fighting, the children were tired and a
little hungry, since the bread supply had not lasted long.

One after the other they went to the single bed they shared —all but Anita, who slept in the bureau drawer.

Sabina, tired of waiting for her husband, finally went to bed. Two things worried her: his absence, the meaning of which she knew only too well, and the baby, who, in the late afternoon, had taken a turn for the worse.

Just as she was falling off to sleep she was roused by loud knocks on the door. She arose and opened it. It was Onofre, dead drunk and unable to stand, accompanied by his friend who held him up. With great difficulty, she undressed him and put him to bed. After all this, she herself was so tired she fell fast asleep, her drunken husband by her side and the baby's face against her bare breast.

Before dawn, she awoke, startled by a queer coldness on her flesh. She sat up and lit the candle. By its light, she discovered that her baby was dead, quite dead.

Without a tear, without a moan, she gazed down for a long time at that face which before had been alive and which now appeared so quiet, so tranquil. As its eyes were still half-open, with her finger she stroked the lids, lowering them until they covered the motionless eyes. Then she put out the light and in that room, lost in shadows, could be heard a soft sobbing which very soon was entirely drowned out by the triumphant orchestration of the drunkard's snores.

THE ABYSS

Rejis picked out his lunch basket, with its little snail shell tied to the handle, from the long line of them against the wall of the mine gallery. He sat between two thick uprights and began to satisfy his voracious appetite, sharpened by five hours of hard labor in the mine.

It was twelve o'clock. The workers of that section were gathering in small groups. The light of the lamps on their visors shone like strange fireflies in the black, winding tunnels.

Each worker, as he reached the line of baskets, took his own, then sought out a corner where he ate his lunch in silence.

For a long quarter hour, all that could be heard beneath that black vault was the muffled chewing and sonorous clinkling of plates and spoons handled by rough, invisible hands.

Suddenly, an isolated voice spoke up, others answered. Soon animated dialogues could be heard in the darkness. At first, the conversation turned on their work, but, little by little, it broadened out to include many subjects. While on one side they discussed seriously in low voices, on the other, they joked and laughed, applauding the banterings of the clowns who invariably chose don Lupe, the oldest man in their gang, as the butt of their jokes. He always arrived last and anxiously searched for his basket, which the pranksters continual-

ly hid from him so that they might shout as he neared
or went away from their hiding place:

"You're hot, don Lupe."

"Cold as the river!"

"Watch out, don Lupe, you're burning!" and they
all laughed uproariously.

Don Lupe was so confused by all this that he just
wandered about aimlessly. Rejis felt sorry for the old
man. He rose and placed the lost basket in his trembling
hands and at the same time he soundly berated the malicious jokers. The latter lost no time replying and from
one end to the other of the dark cavern they hurled on
him a veritable bombardment of gross and vulgar remarks. One of these insults, uttered in an insinuating,
jibing voice, evoked a general burst of howling laughter.

In the darkness, beneath its mask of black coal
dust, Rejis' face turned deathly pale. His first impulse
was to throw himself upon the maligner and punish him
as he deserved for the rotten lie. But a sudden thought
deterred him. He remembered, all at once, a conversation he had overheard by chance that morning:

"So Ramon didn't come down today?"

"I don't believe it!"

"Well, I tell you it's true. Don Pedro asked for
him in the shafthouse and he hadn't even been in to
pick up his tallies."

The suspicion planted in Rejis' mind took seed and
rooted with the speed of a lightning bolt. Could it be
true? The shameful insult that wretch had thrown in
his face? Could she be deceiving him with Ramon? His
face grew drawn and haggard; his eyes burned; he stood
up, tense.

Rejis was twenty years old. His medium height, his
thin body and pale face bespoke the bitter tragedy of a
childhood spent in the depths of the dark tunnels with
no games, no laughter, no air and no sun. Passionately
in love with Delfina, the prettiest and most coquettish

girl in the whole neighborhood, he had won out over all the other suitors who contended for her hand. One of the most tenacious and the last to give up had been Ramon, a boy of his own age, and a formidable opponent indeed, who, in addition to his physical attractions, had ingratiating qualities which made him irresistible to the girls.

In spite of his victory, Rejis lived in fear and dread, for his enemy (piqued by his defeat) had sworn publicly that, sooner or later, he would get what he wanted.

Alone now in the gallery, Rejis tried in vain to calm down. He told himself it was just spiteful gossip. Ramon could be absent for an entirely different reason than that implied by the slanderous tongues of his companions. But his jealousy, so rudely awakened, drowned out his reasoning. His one thought now was to get out of the mine as soon as possible. His mind made up, without even stopping to pick up his lunch basket, he hastened toward the exit. As he went, he elaborated excuses and ways for leaving the mine. It was not easy. On this point the rules of the mine were exceedingly stringent.

The only way would be to feign illness. But besides the revulsion over telling a lie, there was another deterrent here. He would be sent with a mine boss to the infirmary where he would have to be examined by the doctor. This would mean o much delay he would never be able to surprise the culprits.

Driven to desperation by all these difficulties, he was vainly trying to find a way out when, suddenly, a brilliant idea struck him.

He frowned, stopped a second, then turned on his heels and retraced his steps. He hastened through a wide haulageway, skilfully evading the hidden ties that held the slender, steel rails. Suddenly he veered right and entered a very low, narrow, steep manway. Bent double, his hands touching the slimy floor, he climbed laboriously through and finally came out into a passageway that ran parallel to the one he had just left below.

It was an old level, unused now, which communicated
with the shaft hole by an opening thirty metres above
the main haulageway exit.

A few minute's walk brought him to the opening.
Standing on the outjutting rock, he gazed down into
the black depths from which rose the vague murmur of
the muted voices of the workers below. Rejis extinguished
his lamp so that its light would not give him away.
By leaning out a little and stretching his arm, he could
just touch with his fingertips one of the cables on which
the elevator slid. Although his plan was audacious and
extremely dangerous, it was really very simple. Within
a few minutes, the lunch hour over, the whole mine
would be back at work. Once the machinery was in operation again, the elevator below him would carry its load
of coal to the top while the elevator above would bring
down the head overseer. Since the machinery would be
working at minimum velocity, he, if he acted quickly
and calmly, could grab the transverse rod of the ascending cage as it went by. At this hour he was sure of not
finding any of the foremen above and his escape would
go unobserved.

Resolved to try his plan, with every detail firmly
fixed in his mind and every sense alert and ready, he
awaited the exact moment. He could just make out in
the weak light from below the shiny surface of the
thin cable that led to the motionless elevator. Suddenly,
from the shaft, came a very light humming sound. Rejis
moved. He shivered. His practiced ear told him it was
the vibrations of the signal wires to the control room
with their message that all was ready for the ascent.

With bated breath and pounding heart he waited.
A few seconds went by. A light swaying of the cable
announced that the moment for the upward journey was
here. He planted both feet firmly as he could on the
rock, stretched out both arms. He did not have long
now. He barely made out the rising elevator roof. He

lurched forward. His hands hit a hard, smooth surface, slid down a bit, then met an obstacle and grabbed. Instantly he was suspended in a vacuum, wrapped in impenetrable shadows.

But the plan had not worked well. He had miscalculated the speed. Instead of catching hold of the transverse bar, his hands had merely hit the side boards of a coal car and had slipped to the bottom of the cage floor, to a kind of rail the very edge of which his fingers held onto in a claw-like grip.

With infinite horror, Rejis immediately realized the desperateness of his situation. He was overwhelmed with terror, his hair stood on end and his voice strangled in his throat. There was only room in the groove for the first two joints of his twitching fingers. The blood all rushed to his heart when he felt them sliding on the metal, unable to support the violent strain of his body that swung like a pendulum over the abyss. With the terrible muscular effort, it was as though his very flesh were soldering itself into the hard iron. The elevator, with its human trail, rose slowly and evenly up the vertical shaft.

A few very brief instants went by. Rejis could feel the blood beating in his ears and the hammering of his heart in his breast. He began to calculate the distance. How many more metres to the top? To Rejis, with his teeth clenched, eyes bulging, face convulsed and twisted by spasms of agony and bathed in cold sweat, each tenth of a second seemed like an eternity.

Suddenly, to one side, almost brushing him, he half saw something that fell from on high like a stone. A bright light blinded him and he seemed to see a pale face with great, wide-open eyes that shone ominously in the blackness. The two cages as they passed, counterbalancing each other, signaled the point of contact in the customary way. The whistle resounded in Rejis' brain like the shrieking of the four archangels of the Apocalypse screaming in unison:

"You are halfway there! One minute to go, rather a century. One hundred and fifty metres between you and the top, between you and life, between you and safety! Each second that goes by only increases the distance your body will fall as it goes down, down in its dizzying death plunge!"

Rejis was young and vigorous. His entire being, in the very prime of manhood, rebelled against this implacable destiny. No, no! He did not want to die! As his fall became more and more imminent, his spirit took on new, extraordinary vigor. All the past events of his life filed through his mind in a second. Knowing that he could not hold out, that from one moment to the next he was going to have to let go, he almost decided to end the horrible agony. But the thought of the sump cover more than two hundred metres below him drew from him a desperate roar of terror. As though he were on them now, he could see the thick iron planks bristling with pointed nails and spikes, ready to receive and resist the horrible shock of his body hurtled with the force of a cannon ball from two hundred metres above.

Suddenly he felt the fingers of his left hand slipping one after the other over the hard metal. The elevator rose another twenty metres, slow, silent, invisible in the darkness. All at once, Rejis experienced a horrible sensation. The tips of his right hand fingers were sinking, going right through the iron as if the metal were suddenly melting away. For half a second, he hung immobile. Then immediately, a deafening clap of thunder exploded beneath his head. A gust of wind hit his face, cut off his breath.

Half a minute later, the workers at the mouth of the shaft removed from the supplementary platform (which is hung at times from the bottom of the cage to lower large loads into the mine) a miner whose hair was streaked with white, with wide-open, staring eyes and enormous, dilated pupils. Rejis never recovered his reason and he never even knew that whereas he believed he was suspended over a fathomless abyss, not twenty centimetres below the soles of his feet lay a solid oak platform two and a half inches thick.

The printing of this book was completed
on May 10, 1959, in the shops of the
"Editorial Estela," Querétaro 181-B, México
7, D. F. This impression consisted of 2,000
copies in the composition of which the
Medieval and Bodoni types were employed
The illustrations, the design of the dust jacket
and the title pages are the work of *José I.
Bermúdez.*

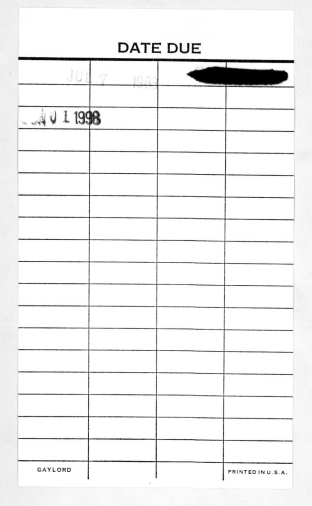

DATE DUE

JUL 7 1965			
JUL 1 1998			
GAYLORD			PRINTED IN U.S.A.